D1302483

The Sky Over Rebecca

The Sky Over Rebecca

MATTHEW FOX

UNION SQUARE KIDS and the distinctive Union Square Kids logo are trademarks of Union Square & Co., LLC.

Union Square & Co., LLC, is a subsidiary of Sterling Publishing Co., Inc.

Text © 2022 Matthew Fox
Illustrations © 2022 Hachette Children's Group

All rights reserved. No part of this publication may be reproduced, stored in a retrieval system, or transmitted in any form or by any means (including electronic, mechanical, photocopying, recording, or otherwise) without prior written permission from the publisher.

ISBN 978-1-4549-5189-6
ISBN: 978-1-4549-5191-9 (paperback)
ISBN: 978-1-4549-5190-2 (e-book)

Library of Congress Cataloging-in-Publication Data

Names: Fox, Matthew, author.
Title: The Sky over Rebecca / Matthew Fox.
Description: New York : Union Square Kids, 2023. | Audience: Ages 8-12. Audience: Grades 4-6. | Summary: Ten-year-old Kara follows mysterious tracks in the snow that lead her across time and space from modern-day Sweden to 1942 Germany where two siblings are hiding from the Nazis.
Identifiers: LCCN 2022061977 (print) | LCCN 2022061978 (ebook) | ISBN 9781454951896 (hardcover) | ISBN 9781454951919 (trade paperback) | ISBN 9781454951902 (epub)
Subjects: CYAC: Space and time—Fiction. | Siblings Fiction. | Jews—Germany—Fiction. | World War, 1939–1945—Fiction. | BISAC: JUVENILE FICTION / Historical / Holocaust | JUVENILE FICTION / Social Themes / Adolescence & Coming of Age | LCGFT: Historical fiction. | Novels.
Classification: LCC PZ7.1.F6917 Sk 2023 (print) | LCC PZ7.1.F6917 (ebook) | DDC [Fic]—dc23
LC record available at https://lccn.loc.gov/2022061977
LC ebook record available at https://lccn.loc.gov/2022061978

For information about custom editions, special sales, and premium purchases, please contact specialsales@unionsquareandco.com.

Printed in the U.S.A.

Lot #:
2 4 6 8 10 9 7 5 3 1

09/23

unionsquareandco.com

llustrations by Ben Mantle

For my mother

and her namesake

One

Somebody had made a snow angel in a perfect white snowdrift down by the lake.

There was something odd about it.

Something about it didn't look right.

I saw it from the window of a bus heading home from town. We were on a bridge, high above the frozen lake. I looked down, and there in the woods on the shore was the snow angel.

There was something strange about it.

I walked home from the bus stop in the last light of the day. It was three o'clock in the afternoon, in early January, and the sun had already set. All around me the city lingered in a gray twilight. Nautical twilight, my grandpa called it, meaning there was still enough light left in the sky for ships to navigate by.

It grew darker.

Lights came on as I approached our building. The snow on the courtyard was pockmarked with three-pronged talons: crows' footprints. Someone had scattered seed here and the crows had eaten it, going back and forth, this way and that, until they'd left a web of tracks in the snow.

I remembered the snow angel.

I saw what was wrong with it.

There had been no footprints. No footprints leading to it, and no footprints leading away from it either.

It was as if someone had dropped out of the sky and lain down in the snow and then vanished.

I looked up at the windows of our apartment, on the seventh floor. They were dark. Lena, my mother, was still at work. She wouldn't be home for another hour or so.

I thought about the snow angel.

I decided to go back.

Two

I got off the bus at the bridge and walked a short way back. The lake was frozen one hundred feet below.

I went down a flight of wooden steps at the side of the road and into the woods. There were street lights here, glowing white, and paths for joggers and dog walkers, and the snow had been thinned out by other people's feet.

I came to a stretch where the streetlights were out, broken, and I turned on the flashlight on my phone. The light fell blue on the snow. The path narrowed and a crow cawed somewhere. The trees looked black and wet. I could hear the sound of my own breathing close by.

Then I stopped.

I was in the clearing.

There was the drift. There was the snow angel.

I shone the light on it.

I was right. There were no footprints leading to it or away from it. The snow was pristine; no one had set foot on it. It was too far from the path for someone to jump, and too far from the trees for someone to climb up and jump down from. And yet someone had lain there, somehow, and stretched out their arms and smoothed out the snow around them to make a pair of wings and a long flowing robe.

The snow angel was deep. The body of it went a foot or so down into the snow. It was as if someone had fallen from a great height and landed slap bang in the middle of the drift. It was as if someone had fallen from the sky.

I looked up. There was nothing up there; nothing you could fall from, anyway. There were just the treetops and the smudged orange glow of the city lights.

There were also crows in the trees, I noticed, all around, black and silent and still. There must have been a hundred of them, come home to roost for the night.

"Hello, crows," I said.

Then I took a photograph of the snow angel on my phone.

There was a sound behind me: a boot crunch on snow. Someone had moved from where they'd been standing watching me—that's what it sounded like, anyway—and I whipped around and aimed the beam of my phone light on the trees behind me. I moved the light, scanning the trees.

"Who's there?" I said.

There was no answer. No one.

"Who's there?" I said again.

This time—when there was no answer—I turned and went quickly back along the path, to home.

Three

There were lights on in the windows of our apartment when I got back. That made me glad. I rode the elevator and let myself in.

My mother was sitting at the kitchen table with her laptop open in front of her, her fingers moving quickly across the keyboard. I came up behind her and we hugged our hellos. I leaned into her and felt the warmth of her, and felt her relax into my embrace.

I could see the screen of the laptop. There was a long list of emails waiting for her there.

"I won't be long," said Mom.

That was almost a lie. I knew it and she knew it too. She'd probably be working all evening and into the night, only getting up from the table to make herself a cup of coffee or to go to the bathroom. But it wasn't a bad lie. She hadn't meant to mislead me. What she'd said was more of a *wish*. She wanted to spend the evening with me. She didn't want to have to work all the time. But the office was, as ever, hectic, and there were always deadlines.

So here she was, at home, with me, but also at work. There was nothing I could do about it.

Still it was good just to be around her. To be in the same room. There was her smell. There was her face. That was something.

I cooked. Vegan sausages and mashed potato. Carrots and parsnips in the mash, too. Lots of herbs (too many herbs; some of them ended up on the floor). Peas on the side, steam rising from them. A little half-bottle of red wine on the table for Mom and a single tall glass.

Tea lights which I lit from a single match.

Then it was ready.

"I sent you an email," I said.

"All right," Mom said. "Let me see."

She opened the email. Attached to it was the photo I'd taken of the snow angel.

"What am I looking at?"

"What do you see?"

"A snow angel."

"Yes," I said, bringing the food to the table.

Then she saw what was odd about it. "No footprints," she said.

"Yes." I sat down facing her.

"Interesting."

Mom closed her laptop and we ate.

"So what do you think?" I said.

"The angel?"

"Yes. How they did it without leaving any footprints."

Mom frowned over her wine glass. "It would take some doing," she said. "It would take some thought."

"You don't know," I said.

"I don't. But I have some ideas."

She couldn't explain it immediately. But she liked a puzzle. While we ate we bounced around ideas about how it could be done. Mom's best suggestion was to tie a strong rope between two trees and climb out along it until you could drop right into the middle of the snowdrift. Then you make the angel, get back on the rope, climb back to the path, untie the rope, and walk away . . .

My best suggestion was being lowered from a helicopter which picked you up again after you'd made the snow angel, but that was really just a joke.

"You'll figure it out," said Mom when we'd run out of ideas.

Somehow we knew we hadn't solved it.

"You'll work it out," Mom said. "I know you will."

It has always been just the two of us. Mom and me. We've always been together.

I've read about children in books going off on adventures looking for their real parents but I don't need to go anywhere. My real parent is right here, sitting across from me now while we eat, and she's pretty good at this parenting thing, despite the laptop open on the kitchen table.

There is no other parent. No one is missing. There's no one to go looking for and I don't even have an interesting story to tell about why there's no one to go looking for.

What happened was my father met someone else shortly after I was born. Someone he wanted to be with more than he wanted to be with us. He moved away to another country, where he married again, and Mom and I changed our names.

We went back to my mother's family name, Lukas. I'm glad about that. Lukas is a very old name from the Latin word *lux*, meaning *light*. It's a good name to have if you live in the dark, which we do most of the time in winter.

We live in Stockholm, in Sweden. It's on the same latitude as Alaska, which is pretty far north as far as this planet goes. In summer the days are long, so long they never seem to want to end. It's light long before you get up in the morning and it's still light long after you go to bed. But in winter the world turns dark, and it's the nights that grow long, and longer, and the days kind of curl up into themselves, as if even they don't want to brave the cold and the dark.

Meanwhile, the snow falls.

And falls.

And falls.

And everything freezes, even the lake I can see from my bedroom window, the great lake, Lake Mälaren. When a lake like that freezes it stays frozen for months. It's like it's been turned to stone. You can walk on it. Jump up and down on it. Skate on it. And I do. Except—

Except I don't trust it.

I don't trust Mälaren.

Something about it scares me.

Mom says it's because I nearly drowned there when I was little. Maybe. I don't know, I don't remember. I was three years old. I walked out on the ice by myself. Mom was there, on the shore, with my grandpa, David Lukas. But they were distracted. The ice cracked and I slipped straight in. I screamed, and my mouth filled with lake water and I disappeared.

Grandpa, who was old then, and who is now even older, walked out onto the lake to get me. He let the ice break under his feet until he was wading through the sludge toward me. It came all the way up to his shoulders.

I was underwater the whole time.

Grandpa reached down into the dark water and pulled me up by the scruff of my neck.

I coughed up lake water.

Grandpa carried me back to shore.

I vomited. I was in the hospital for two nights.

I don't remember any of it.

The landline rang while we were having dinner. That could only be one person: Grandpa. He still didn't own a cell phone, and he was the only person I knew who actually *took out a pen and wrote down* people's telephone numbers in a little black book he carried around with him.

I got up from the table and answered the phone.

"Grandpa?"

"How did you know it was me?" he said, although he was laughing as he said it—I could hear it in his voice—and then he said, "Seriously now, Kara. You may be able to see the Quadrantids tonight. Even in Stockholm. There have been sightings."

Meteors. The Quadrantids were a meteor shower. They fall in late December and early January.

"Have you seen them?" I asked.

"They're not here yet," he said, "but I've spoken to a friend of mine at the Observatory. They're on their way."

"I hope you get to see them."

"You too."

"I'll look for them," I said.

"Good. Put your mother on, would you?"

"Goodnight, Grandpa," I said.

"Goodnight, Kara."

I handed Mom the phone and went back to my food. She and Grandpa spoke for a long while. I couldn't hear what Grandpa was saying, only Mom's side of it, which was mostly "Yes, I see," and "Yes, I understand . . ."

I wondered what they were talking about. Grandpa hadn't been too well recently. He'd been in the hospital with an infection and recovered, but while he was there they'd found some strange rhythms in his heart. The timings were wrong. It was something he could live with, the doctors said, but it was also something that might simply spirit him away one night.

I made coffee for Mom and loaded the dishwasher and set it running quietly.

Mom opened her laptop and went back to work. She would work on into the night.

I had falling stars to see.

Four

Grandpa had been decluttering. One of the things he'd decluttered was a telescope. It was old. It had been his when he was a boy. He thought I might like it.

He was right. I did.

It was on the desk by the window in my room. On the windowsill behind it was an old cardboard planisphere that had also been Grandpa's.

A planisphere is a circular map of the stars you can adjust for the time of year. I know that's a strange idea—an adjustable map—but that's what it is.

I turned the cardboard wheel inside the planisphere to today's date. That showed what I should have been able to see in the sky, looking north. Then I turned out the lights and waited for my eyes to get used to the dark.

I leaned on the windowsill and looked at the apartment buildings below us on the side of the hill. There were six buildings there. They were each as high as ours, seven floors, but because they were built on the slope going down to the lake they seemed to be all different heights. From my window I could see the rooftops of all the buildings and some of the apartments, and what the people who lived in them were up to.

I watched the people for a while. I should say I wasn't spying on them. I wasn't trying to find out anything about them. I wasn't even really being nosy. I didn't even know them. I just looked at their lives for a few moments and then looked away. There were families down there: small children in their pajamas ready for bed; teenagers playing computer games on TVs as big as walls; adults cooking, chopping vegetables while saucepans steamed and the windows fogged up.

Above them all, there was snow on all the rooftops of the apartment buildings. It was deep and had been swept flat by the wind off the lake.

On one of the rooftops, however, the snow was not quite pristine. Something had been up there. Or someone.

It looked like footprints.

I went from the window to the telescope and angled it down and put my eye to the eyepiece. Then I reeled in the focus, spinning the wheel, and looked at the rooftop.

I was right.

There were footprints in the snow on the roof.

It looked like someone had walked across the roof of the apartment building. They started at the peak and walked down the shallow slope to the edge that hung out over the gutters.

This wasn't particularly strange in itself. This is Sweden; it snows, and the snow has to be cleared off the rooftops in case it slides off and lands on people walking below. You can be sued if people get hurt that way. So all the apartment buildings here pay crews of people to go up on the roofs and sweep the snow off.

Probably whoever had been up there was doing some essential maintenance. Probably they'd have had a safety rope and a crash helmet.

I tilted the telescope upward and looked at the sky.

I turned the focus wheel slowly, looking for something out there.

Clear sky.

No moon.

But I could see only two or three stars: only the very brightest. The rest of the sky was dark. I was looking in the right place, using the right focal length. But there was nothing else to see.

That was pretty much as I expected. I live in a city.

Cities have lights.

The light bleeds into the sky.

All the electric lights burning in all the windows of all the apartments. All the streetlights and the blinking neon advertisements. All the headlights and the taillights on all the vehicles on all the roads snaking through the city. It was a living map of light as far as the eye could see. So light, so bright, you couldn't even see the stars.

Astronomers call this skyglow.

It was worth looking for the Quadrantids, the meteors Grandpa had called to tell me about. I'm always willing to wait for a good meteor shower, and they should be the brightest thing in the sky. Sometimes the light pollution thins out in the upper atmosphere. Sometimes the air itself is clearer, depending on the wind, and you can see more of the planets and more stars outside our solar system.

While I waited for the meteors, something happened.

I got lucky.

I got seriously lucky.

Five

The lights went out.

First one by one, building by building, and then all at once, the lights of the city went out. Great patches of dark appeared in the quilt of light, and spread, and ran into other patches of dark, and a great dark wave rolled in toward the city center, which went under into blackness and silence. The wave rolled on, toward the lake, across the bridge. I saw everything: the windows in the apartments going dark; the streetlights blinking out. Then the wave reached us, on the south side of the lake, and I saw the apartment buildings down the hill from us go dark.

It was a power cut.

Some minor fault somewhere deep underground, perhaps.

Gradually, the sky above the city was filled with a different kind of light.

The stars came out.

I looked through the telescope.

The Quadrantids were coming down, great chunks of ice and stone from millions upon millions of miles away. They fell silently, burning up in our atmosphere, glowing blue and white and green.

I watched them fall.

The meteor shower was beautiful and I watched it for a long time. Then I turned the focus wheel carefully, taking the depth all the way out, past the showering meteors, past the planets, past the stars in our own galaxy.

I looked at the stars in the constellation of Andromeda.

It was like a mist of light.

A cluster of stars—a galaxy—like a pearl.

Then Andromeda disappeared.

The blackout was over. The lights came on.

The stars faded away.

I looked out of the window and watched a steady wave of light rolling in across the land. Everything was on, again: all the streetlights, all the neon advertisements, all the lights in all the windows of the apartments.

I looked at the apartments below us on the side of the hill and saw the people in the windows come to life again with the light. Then I looked at the footprints on the roof, and I noticed something strange.

There were more footprints.

The earlier set of footprints had come down the slope of one roof to the very edge.

But the new set of footprints didn't stop there. They continued, on to the roof of the next building, twenty yards away, without missing a beat. It was as if the walker had simply stepped out into thin air and walked on, across the dark gap to the next roof.

In between it was a sheer drop.

Twenty yards to the ground.

You'd need wings, I thought.

Six

In the morning the footprints were gone.

It was light already; I'd slept late, wrestling with strange dreams. Then I opened the curtains and looked for the footprints.

There were workmen on the rooftops today, clearing the snow. They wore bright red uniforms and brighter helmets, and they moved with ropes across the slopes of the roofs. They used broad brushes and wide spades to shift the snow.

Great slabs of snow fell silently through the air and exploded on the courtyards and paths below, where other workmen stood watch in case anyone was walking directly underneath.

They'd already cleared the snow from the rooftops where I'd seen the footprints.

There was no evidence anybody had ever been up there.

I went through to the kitchen. Mom had gone to work already. I wouldn't see her again until late tonight.

I'd be alone again, all day.

Some terrible feeling rose up in me then.

It's a feeling I've had sometimes before.

Recently I've been having it more often.

It's like a cold wind blowing through you.

Somehow, having clothes doesn't seem to help. There aren't enough layers in the world. The wind rattles the bones in your body anyway.

Adults call this depression.

I call it loneliness.

Yesterday, for example, I didn't talk to anyone all day. Not until I saw the snow angel, and that's when I started talking to you. There was something strange about the snow angel and I needed to talk to somebody about it if I was going to figure it out. So I started talking to you. But before that I didn't speak to anyone.

What I did yesterday was I got a bus, and then a train, and went to the Mall of Scandinavia. That's where I stayed, all day, on the off chance that I'd see somebody I knew from school and have someone to talk to. So I went in the shops and looked at the clothes, and sat in a coffee shop and reread my old, battered copy of *Tom's Midnight Garden*, and later I sat for a long time on a bench next to some old people.

But I didn't see anybody I knew all day.

The truth is I'm not good at making friends. It's not something I have the skills for. I don't know how to do it. I don't know what to say to people.

So instead I feel a cold wind blowing through me, raging, and I wonder if anybody cares about me.

Anybody in the world.

I waited for the feeling to subside.

That was what you had to do. Stay on your feet. Keep breathing. Wait, and the feeling will pass.

The cold wind inside slowed, and sighed, and ceased.

I began to feel like I could make it through the day.

I made myself some oatmeal with raisins and honey.

I sat down and started to eat.

The telephone rang then—the landline.

Grandpa.

I raced over and picked up the phone.

It was him.

He wanted to know what I was doing today.

He wanted to know if I wanted to go skating.

Seven

From where we live to the lake is roughly half a mile. We live in an old apartment building on the top of a hill, although when I say hill what I mean is rock. Stockholm is made of rocks sticking up out of the water.

Below us on the side of the rock that slopes down to the lake are the new apartment buildings, where I saw the footprints on the roof. These are modern buildings, all built within the last ten years. There are stairs and paved pathways between the buildings and ornamental gardens and a play area with swings, although right now everything is under the snow.

To get from our block to the new buildings you go down an old, uneven flight of stone steps. Nobody knows how old these steps are, or who made them, or why. But once upon a time somebody carved them out of solid rock.

I remember a girl at school saying that the Vikings made the old steps here, and I don't know whether that's true or not, but the idea got stuck in my head, and that's what I've always called them: the Viking Steps.

From the steps you go along past a row of old garages and around and down the stairways and paths that thread through the new apartment buildings. It's a maze if you don't know where you're going. You have to go first one way and then another. Then to go straight ahead you have to go sideways. But you do eventually plop out at the bottom of the complex, right into the woods.

These woods aren't anything like the woods where I saw the snow angel.

These woods are different.

These woods are dark.

Once upon a time there was a dispute about who owned the land beneath these woods, and the dispute rumbles and rankles on to this day. In the meantime, nobody can touch anything or change anything or build anything down there.

There are no streetlights. The trees grow old and they keep on growing, older than Mom, older even than Grandpa, and the paths appear wherever people walk and keep on walking.

Today the paths were invisible under the snow. I went my own way down through the woods. There were no other people I could see. No runners or dog walkers. I was alone, and the air tasted clean and the silence felt pure.

Every step I took was a new crunch, a new mark on the surface of the world.

I sang a song to myself quietly. No one could hear me. I walked and I sang.

The way ahead was all windswept snow and dark leafless trees that curled up and met overhead. The branches had become entangled up there, darkening the path and making it a little like a tunnel of trees.

Up the middle of this tunnel there was a single trail of footprints, the first I'd seen all morning.

I walked alongside the footprints for a while. They were fresh tracks, I saw, the edges of the impressions in the snow quite hard.

Small feet. Like mine.

Someone my age.

Then they stopped.

They stopped in midair, or rather, in mid-stride.

They stopped and they didn't continue.

It was as if the person whose footprints these were had suddenly taken flight and walked on without so much as touching the ground.

It was the kind of detail you might not normally notice. It was the kind of thing you might have to have pointed out to you, to make you see how strange it was.

I noticed these things because I was lonely.

I had too much time on my hands.

I spent more time looking at nature than I did at people, which was probably a mistake if I wanted to make friends.

I stared at the footprints on the ground.

I looked back along the tree tunnel.

I wondered if someone was playing tricks on me.

The possibility that someone was watching me, secretly, and laughing at me, made me hurry on.

I went down to the lake.

I strapped on my skates.

Grandpa was already out there on the ice.

He waved.

Eight

We skated for an hour. I was on blades, Grandpa on short skis. We worked the ice with Nordic ski poles for extra stability.

Black-and-gray crows watched us from high above, wondering what on earth we were doing down there on the hard, white water.

We didn't speak. We just skated.

There were other people out on the ice, too. We crossed paths every now and then and said our hellos, and went on our ways.

The sound of our skates on the ice was soothing.

Grandpa looked at his watch.

"I'm getting tired," he said.

On the other side of the lake was a kiosk that sold hot dogs and fries and ice cream. The man behind the counter knew us from winters past, and waved hello as we unclipped our skates and came over.

His name was Abdul and he was Persian. He'd come to Sweden as a refugee in the late 1970s. Now he was a grandpa himself, with Swedish grandchildren who went to the same school as me.

He knew what we were going to order before we opened our mouths: vegan hot dogs with lots of ketchup and mustard, a cup of coffee, a can of Julmust.

Grandpa paid for the food, and we sat down on a bench nearby and ate. Only then did I see how tired he was. He was old, astronomically old, and he still lived by himself in an old house about ten miles outside the city. He was fast on skis, out there on the ice, but on dry land you could see how careful he was when he moved, and that he kept a close watch on where he put his feet.

We hadn't been out on the lake as much this winter.

We ate our hot dogs in silence. I sensed there was something Grandpa wanted to say to me but couldn't—not yet.

Perhaps he'd decided it could wait.

I could wait, too. So instead, when we'd eaten our hot dogs and Grandpa had gone back for a refill of his coffee, we spoke about the stars.

I can't remember when Grandpa first told me about the stars. What they were. How far away they were. How big the universe might be.

It feels like I've always known they're suns, like our sun, only much, much farther away.

But I do remember the moment I understood what that meant. I remember we were at Grandpa's house, in the garden. It was an autumn night and the sky was clear. Stockholm was only a distant glow to the east.

The stars were luminous.

There were so many of them.

The universe was so big and we were so small.

The universe was immense beyond anything you could imagine. Untold distances surpassing untold distances. It was too vast even for light: even light wasn't fast enough to flash across the distances involved.

Even light found itself alone, rolling through the vast empty spaces of the universe.

"There," Grandpa said, pointing, "Andromeda."

He was holding my hand.

The pearl.

Grandpa told me then how far away the Andromeda Galaxy was: two and a half million light years away. Which meant we were looking at Andromeda as it was two and a half million years ago. That was how long the light it had emitted once, long ago, had taken to reach us.

We were looking back in time.

"We can see them, but they can't see us," Grandpa had said. "As far as they're concerned, we don't exist. We haven't been born yet."

And if, at this very moment, there were people living on one of the planets in the Andromeda Galaxy, and they were looking at Earth through a very powerful telescope, what they'd see was the Earth as it was two and a half million years ago.

They wouldn't see me, or Grandpa. They wouldn't see Sweden or the light from our cities or even the pyramids.

They wouldn't see humans. We hadn't arrived yet.

They might see our ancestors, Australopithecus, in Africa. They might see our ancestors looking up at the moon and the stars, and watching meteors fall, and looking back at an even older Andromeda in the sky.

They might see our ancestors wondering who was up there, watching them.

Grandpa squeezed my hand.

That autumn, Grandpa had still been well. He had not so much as spent a single night in the hospital in his life until then. But time had passed. Time had set to work on a very old man. He had been in and out of the hospital a couple of times since then.

Which is what he wanted to talk about, I think, out on the lake that day.

His death.

What happens afterward.

How Mom and I will get by once he's gone.

But the moment never came, and Grandpa never said what was on his mind. He finished his coffee and looked at his watch. "I'm cold," he said.

There was a bus stop a short walk from the kiosk and a bus waiting there, and I ran to hold it for Grandpa while he walked steadily behind. We hugged good-bye, and then he was gone and I turned to skate back across the lake, to the wild woods.

Nine

I came back through the tunnel of trees where I'd seen the footprints earlier.

More people had been here as the day had gone on, and dogs too, leaving many tracks and turning the path to slush, and I could no longer work out which were the first set of footprints and which came later.

The mystery had been erased.

But I saw something else on the ground, in the slush, while I stood there and looked.

It was a coin.

Small and half-buried in gray snow. I took off my glove and reached for it, and brushed off the snow and held it in my hand.

It was the strangest coin I have ever seen.

It felt light, almost as if it could float out of my hand. It wasn't made of the sort of things they made coins out of these days, but of some much cheaper metal. And there was a date stamped on it,1942, although somehow it didn't appear to be worn down for a coin that old.

I could make out the word "*Pfennig.*"

On one side of the coin was a big "5." On the other side there was an eagle.

Underneath the eagle was a swastika.

I knew what that was. I knew what that meant.

I knew where this coin was from.

It was from Germany—but not the Germany of today. This was from an older Germany, a very different Germany.

I heard whispering then, and a boot crunch on snow.

I looked around, and just as I did—

Whoomph!

Something hit me right in the face.

A snowball.

Whoomph!

Another snowball. Just missing me.

Then—*Whoomph!*—another one—in my face.

Four boys were coming through the trees. They had more snowballs ready in their hands.

I knew them from school. They were the last people I wanted to see these holidays.

More snowballs were incoming. I got up and ran and I got splattered with snow.

I could hear them laughing behind me.

The rain of snowballs stopped. They were reloading. Scooping up more snow and packing it tight and hard and cold.

I dropped down behind a tree and peered back through the undergrowth.

I knew one of the boys. Well, I knew all of them—their faces. But I knew one of the boys by name.

Lars.

He was twelve, I think. The year above me. Blond like so many Swedes, while I was dark-haired and different. He didn't like me, I don't think, although we'd never so much as exchanged two words with each other.

Worse, he lived near me, in one of the new apartment buildings on the side of the hill going down to the lake. Which meant we were always bumping into each other or waiting at the same bus stop or finding ourselves on the same bus home and just ignoring each other.

I didn't like him.

But he was the leader of the pack.

I watched him now, pressing a piece of stone into a snowball. A cold black flint that would hurt if it got you.

That's not right, I thought.

Stones aren't fair.

I grabbed a handful of snow and packed it tight.

Snowballs hurtled through the air toward me.

I aimed—and threw my snowball.

Lars missed with his—the stone whacked into a tree.

But my aim was good.

My snowball hit Lars—*SMACK!*—in the face.

More snowballs rained down but I didn't move. I just stood there for a moment and watched Lars turn bright red. Seething with fury and embarrassment.

Our eyes met across the drift.

I turned and ran. Fast as I could. I knew my way back through the woods and I went this way and that, and I came to a well-worn path. Behind me, Lars and his pack were chasing after me. I could hear their shouts. I could hear their feet in the snow.

I ran on. There were dog walkers coming the other way, toward me, and two dogs were off their leashes, big black dogs. They barked at me as I ran toward them but I just kept on, and behind me I heard the dogs going absolutely nuts. Four boys were sprinting toward them and the dogs thought it was all a fantastic game, and I looked back and saw Lars pinned to a tree by the largest of the dogs, paws on his chest, and its owner was trying to pull it away.

I ran on and came to the new apartment buildings. They weren't following me now and I slowed to a walk. I was sweating under my winter clothes. I climbed the Viking Steps, out of breath and red in the face.

There would be trouble the next time I saw Lars. I'd better be prepared to run. He was bigger than me. And he'd been in fights: I'd seen one of them, at school, a real fight with kicking and punching, and the other boy had started crying afterward.

The crying had been a mistake, I thought.

Don't cry, whatever you do.

Don't let them see you cry.

I'd made a different kind of mistake with the snowball that had hit him right in the face, hadn't I?

I would just have to avoid him now.

I was home.

I let myself into the lobby.

My breath came back to me slowly.

Then I took off my gloves.

I still had the coin.

The coin with the eagle and the swastika on it.

I must have put it in my glove for safekeeping just as the snowballs started to fall.

Ten

There were no lights on in the apartment when I got home.

I went straight to my room. The sun had set on the lake below, but up here on the seventh floor, on the top of the hill, the sun was still setting in the west.

I didn't turn a light on. I let the last rays of the sun stream into my room. I sat on the bed and looked at the coin I'd found in the snow.

Someone had lost it in the snow.

But why would anybody have such a coin these days?

You couldn't spend it anymore. It was worthless, and in any event the country that minted these coins had been defeated, long ago.

It belonged in a museum, not in somebody's pocket.

Why would anybody want a coin with a swastika on it?

Because you know what that means.

You know it, and I know it.

I know where this coin is from.

I know what happened there.

Six million people were murdered.

Six million children and adults were murdered because they were Jews, and for no other reason.

It was called the Holocaust.

I stared at the swastika on the coin.

I ran my finger over the slightly raised edge.

Outside, the last rays of the sun were dimming down to nothing.

I looked up at the shelf on the other side of the room. There was a tin box up there full of odds and ends. It had been my mother's when she was a child, an old cookie tin, with a faded colored pattern showing men and women walking through a fairground.

I could keep the coin there.

I took the tin down from the shelf and opened it. There were all sorts of childish things inside, all sorts of things I'd forgotten I even owned: some marbles, a pocketknife, an old tin whistle on a piece of string, some Danish coins with holes in them, a plastic magnifying glass, three pencils, and some stones I'd collected, long ago, from a beach in the south of Sweden.

I put the coin in there along with the other bits and pieces and I took the whistle out. I blew on it once (it made a good sound) and I put the string over my head and let it hang there around my neck. For some reason it made me feel calm. Then I closed the tin and put it back on the shelf.

The sun was gone.

It was dark in my room.

Still I didn't put a light on. I just sat there in the dark. I needed to think about what had happened.

Images flickered through my mind: a snow angel, footprints in the snow on the rooftops, a coin with a terrible history . . .

Lars.

Perfect blond Lars.

That was going to be whatever it was going to be. There was nothing I could do about that. I just had to avoid him until he'd forgotten about me and settled on a new victim.

Then there was Grandpa.

Grandpa and the something he wasn't telling me.

I turned my head. There was the telescope he'd given me, on the desk below the window.

I got up and went to the telescope.

I put my eye to the eyepiece.

I turned the focus wheel.

I looked at the rooftops of the apartment buildings where I'd seen the footprints last night. There was nothing there now, just a dusting of fresh snow that had fallen during the day.

I turned the telescope slowly and tilted it down.

There was Lars, walking back from the bus stop, alone. He lived somewhere around here, in one of the newer apartment buildings on the hill below us. It would be good to know which one, I thought, then I could avoid him. So I tracked him with the telescope, through the streets and along the little paths, and after losing him behind one of the buildings, I found him again at the door of another, and I watched him enter the door code and go inside.

I turned the telescope to the west, past the apartment buildings. I trained it on the woods down by the lake.

There were no streetlights down there. The snow was a pale white-blue. The gloom seemed to hover a few feet off the ground amidst a tangle of black branches.

I turned the focus wheel. The image sharpened and I found a trail of footprints in the snow. It took me a moment to realize they were my footprints; they were the tracks I'd made this morning when I cut through the woods on my way down to the lake.

It felt strange, seeing my own tracks like that. To see my footprints, alone in a dense dark wood, and so far away from me now. It felt like I was looking back in time.

It felt lonely.

I stared at my footprints for a while. The wind came through the trees, shifting the snow a little, and settled again. It was a cold night out there.

Presently I saw somebody out there.

Somebody was coming along the path I'd made.

Somebody was walking in my footsteps.

It was a girl.

Eleven

The telescope magnified everything. I could see details. I could see the bark of the trees. I could see crows ruffling their feathers in the branches above.

I could see her face. The face of the girl who came along the path through the woods, walking in my footsteps.

She was my age or a little older. Dark hair, darker than mine. Her skin looked almost blue in the cold, and haunted. Her coat, an overcoat, was two sizes too big for her, and worn out. Her gloves—mittens—looked too thin for this weather.

I wondered what she was doing out in such cold.

She was bound to catch her death.

In the pockets of the old overcoat she carried a few sticks or twigs or old bits of wood. Every now and then as she walked along she stopped to pick up another piece of wood or fallen branch just lying there in the snow. I watched her as she went about her collecting. It was not long before she had a bundle of branches under her arm, and her pockets were stuffed full of sticks.

Firewood, I thought.

She's collecting wood for a fire.

She stopped in front of a great untouched bank of snow. Then she came to some decision, and set her bundle on the ground and walked into the snowdrift.

She lay on her back.

Spread out her arms.

Smoothed out all the snow that lay within reach.

And made a perfect snow angel.

She stood up, dusted herself off, and walked back to the path. I wondered how she was going to get rid of her footprints leading to and from the angel—but it was a fleeting thought. She looked at the angel and seemed pleased with what she'd done, and turned and picked up her bundle of wood, and went on her way.

I followed her every move.

She went down to the lake.

Mälaren was a shadowy white emptiness amidst the dark gray of the night. The lights of the city glowed faintly there, reflected in its opaque surface.

A small figure appeared, walking out across the ice. The girl. No skates on her feet. No skis. Just boots with studs probably, or spikes; enough grip under them to keep her upright. On she went, the bundle of wood under her arm. Walking farther out on the ice, westward, away from the city to the darker areas beyond, but with some clear destination in mind.

The darkness swirled around her.

What could be out there? I thought.

What was out there, in the middle of the lake?

A dark distant shape I had taken for a patch of black ice resolved itself into something else.

An island.

An island in the middle of the lake.

An island I'd never really noticed before.

But there it was, and there she was.

The girl came to the island. I watched her step ashore and disappear into the trees.

I watched, and waited, until I saw it.

The low red glow of a fire almost hidden in the trees.

So I was right about the branches and the sticks and the twigs. She'd been collecting it to make a fire. And this was where she was staying the night.

My first thought was that she was on some kind of survival course from school or Scouts or something like that. Like this was a test and it was all properly supervised, and everybody was insured and things like that.

But her clothes, I thought.

Her clothes had been threadbare.

This is not normal, I thought.

This was something *desperate* and *sad* and *awful*.

I had to find out more about her.

Twelve

There was a storm in the night. A real blizzard, with the wind still whistling around the building when I woke up and more snow on top of everything that had fallen already.

It was still snowing when I opened the curtains and looked out on the lake, and that's when I remembered the girl I'd seen through the telescope last night.

The girl in the woods.

The girl on the island.

The telescope was where I'd left it the night before. I put my eye to the eyepiece, and there was the island, blurry and far away, sitting out the storm. Snow fell around it, and the wind whipped drifts around it, and the trees that clung to the rocks on the shore there shivered and swayed in the air.

There was nothing on the island. Nobody lived there, I decided, because nobody could live there. Nobody could spend the night out there in a storm like this. Nobody could survive there on their own.

I thought about the girl.

Was she real?

I wasn't so sure now.

Had I imagined her?

One thing that was real was the coin I'd found in the snow. That was undeniably real.

I wanted to know more about it. I wanted to know why it was here.

Thirteen

I went out into the storm. The air was full of snow, coming at you from every direction: there was no avoiding it and I made a run for the bus stop and sheltered there.

I took a bus into the city, to the Old Town and the waterfront.

The Baltic Sea churned choppy and green in the harbor, and rusty buoys swayed and rose and fell in the winter water. Farther out, a cruise ship as tall as an apartment building was moored: it was an island of its own making, complete with captive islanders. There were stick figures at the windows of all the decks, and I wondered if the vacationers felt trapped, or if they were secretly enjoying the storm.

I walked up to the Old Town where the tall, narrow streets offered some protection from the storm. I turned a corner and there was the old antique shop I had come here for, looking even more run-down than I remembered. Some gloom clung to it, and to the wet, cobbled street it was in, and both the street and the shop remained in shadow through all the hours of the day, even in summer.

A sign in the door said OPEN. But the sign was an old piece of card, much-thumbed, and the display in the window was cluttered and dusty. Nothing had been changed in years. And yet, in amongst the ugly pieces of bone china on the purple drapes there were some coins, old coins, from all over Europe, and that's why I had come here, to find out more about the coin.

The German coin.

I put my hand to the dull brass door handle and went in. An old metal bell above the door clanged once and I closed the door behind me.

Inside there was gloom and a smell: dust and age, and something unhealthy, like black mold, or some damp that had been allowed to go untreated for years.

I looked around. There were many things in the shop: old things, weird things, ugly things. Tables, chairs, and bits and pieces of crockery, none of it matching, none of it easy on the eye. Garish colors had been preserved by a lack of direct sunlight.

Above all this junk were the clocks. A dozen or so clocks, old clocks, wooden and brass, around the walls, and in the stillness that swallowed me when I entered, I could hear the clocks ticking.

I went to the counter. It was covered with worn, greenish glass. Through the glass I could see more old coins in presentation cases below. They looked like they were underwater.

Behind the counter was a workbench, and behind the workbench was a flight of wooden steps leading down into the private part of the shop.

After a moment there was a *pitter-patter* sound, and a small dog came up the short flight of stairs from the back, and stopped and looked at me. It cocked its head. Then it turned and went back down again.

Shortly afterward an old man came shuffling up the same stairs to the counter. He had long white hair that came down loosely to his shoulders. He was too old to still be working in a shop, I thought. Not because old people can't work, of course, or shouldn't, but because he'd been struggling on the steps. He had a walking stick with him. He looked tired and winced as he put the walking stick to one side. But when he turned to look at me through his round glasses I saw that he was not out of breath, and his voice was surprisingly firm.

"No kids," he said.

"I just have a question," I said.

"No questions," came the reply.

"I found this," I said.

I opened the handkerchief I'd carried the coin in.

There was the coin.

Swastika side up.

The old man saw it. He had been about to say something else. The words *get out* had been on the tip of his tongue. But he managed to stop himself. His eyes, behind his glasses, widened and sharpened and focused.

He picked up a pair of gloves from behind the counter, thin white cotton gloves, but clean, and put them on. Then he reached out a hand toward the coin.

"May I?"

"Yes."

He took the coin and held it up to his eyes, studying it, squinting. He raised and lowered his glasses. They were bifocals, I noticed.

"It's light," I said. "It doesn't weigh anything."

"Yes," he said. "Zinc. Cheap metal. It was the war. The old war. They saved the heavier, stronger metals for bullets and bombs."

"It has a swastika on it."

"Yes."

He turned away then. On the workbench behind the counter were magnifying lenses and little bright lights and some fine metal tools.

The old man put the coin on the workbench. He swung a large magnifying glass over it and clicked on a light. He began to study the coin, massively enlarged.

While he worked, he said, "What is your name?"

"Kara Lukas," I said.

"Kara. My name is Albert Breck."

"Hi, Albert," I said.

Albert *hmmmed* to himself. He was puzzled by the coin.

"Germany," he said. "Nineteen forty-two."

"I know that."

"Yes," he said. "It's genuine. But it looks brand new . . . I don't understand it. Unless this has come from a private collection."

He turned to look at me now, over his glasses.

"Where did you say you found it?"

"Mälaren," I replied.

"The lake?"

"Yes."

"The lake," said Albert to himself. Right then he seemed to go into some kind of trance. He still had the coin in his hand, but now he closed his fingers, forming a fist around the German coin, as if to crush it. All the while he stared into space over my head with his mouth slightly open, as if he were about to say something else.

He was in the grip of a memory. Something had stirred. Some unbidden memory, something to do with the lake, or something to do with the coin, had come back to him.

Eventually I coughed into my sleeve.

Albert didn't react.

I coughed again, louder, and now he looked at me.

It was as if he'd never been away.

"Whereabouts?" he said. "Where, on the lake?"

"The wild woods," I replied. "West of the city."

Albert nodded as if he knew the exact spot I was talking about.

"May I have the coin back?" I said.

He opened his fist and looked at the coin in the palm of his hand.

"Yes," he said. "You may have it back. In two days."

"In two days?"

"Yes. Because I am going to find out how much this is worth for you. Would you like that?"

"I suppose so," I said. It was not something I'd thought about. All I'd been able to think about was the swastika.

"You're under no obligation to sell," he said. "But if you do sell, I would be happy to arrange a buyer."

He wrote something on an old pad with a piece of blue carbon paper under the top sheet, and stamped it. Then he tore off the top copy and handed it to me.

"Here is your receipt," he said. "Bring this with you when you come back."

Fourteen

I went home, and stayed in for the rest of the day, sitting reading on the windowsill, looking up every now and then from my book to watch the storm rage over the city.

It was quietly thrilling being inside—reading a story about children traveling in time—and being safe behind the windows while the hail and the stinging rain whipped around the building and battered the woods down below.

By mid-afternoon it had blown itself out.

The skies cleared and the sun appeared low over the lake, as if to say, *Here I am, I haven't forgotten about you; here, have some light.*

Then it went down.

I thought about the girl I'd seen in the woods. If she was real.

And if she was real, and not just somebody I'd made up, she'd be venturing out now that the storm was over. If she lived out there, alone, on the island, there would be wood to collect for a fire, to keep her warm through the long, dark night to come.

I put my eye to the telescope and looked at the wild woods, but there was no one there: only snow and crows.

Then I looked at the lake, and there she was.

A lone figure, walking across the great expanse of ice. She was hauling wood for a fire again, headed for the island. But when she arrived, she put her bundle of wood down and took off her boots. Then from some hiding place she took out a pair of red skates.

She put them on and stepped out on to the ice.

She skated, nervously at first, but with increasing confidence. I followed her every move.

I saw her elegance.

I watched her episodic loops and curls.

I smiled, watching her.

She curled away and came swinging back, curled away again and came swinging back again, and then she whipped round and drew back, and I saw that she had scored a figure eight in the ice.

Infinity.

I looked at my watch. Mom wouldn't be home for a couple of hours yet.

I had time to go down to the lake.

I could meet this strange girl.

I could get to know her.

I checked the battery on my phone. I had a full charge, which was good because the battery was not very reliable in the cold. Sometimes if the temperature was below zero it just decided to stop working, and I needed it to work if I was going to go out on the lake. It's not that I had anybody to call; nor that anybody was likely to call me. It was more about the light: I'd need to use it.

The woods were dark. The lake was dangerous. I hadn't been down there in the dark on my own before.

I grabbed my skates and my big coat and waterproof boots and went down in the elevator and stepped out into the dark.

I skated out on the ice. I came to the island.

There was no sign of the girl I'd seen.

The island itself seemed empty. There weren't even any crows roosting in the bare trees, and there are always crows.

I wondered for a moment if I'd imagined the girl.

I skated on a little way and came to the proof beneath my feet. There were fresh cuts and score marks in the ice. I turned on the light on my phone and there it was: the infinity symbol.

It wasn't just my imagination.

From out of the dark came the sound of skates on ice. In the cold air it sounded like the wind, like a whistle, so high-pitched it came and went in your ears and you were never sure what direction it was coming from.

Then I saw the skater.

She came out of the gloom.

It was her.

It was the girl.

Fifteen

She slowed as she came toward me and stopped.

She was looking directly at me, standing about thirty feet away on the ice.

She had a strange expression on her face. She was looking at me but also kind of through me. It was as if she weren't quite sure who or what I was, or even if I was really there at all.

"Hello," I said.

She didn't say anything. She just turned her head a little to the side, as if she'd heard something, distantly, but couldn't place where the sound was coming from.

"Hey," I said. "Are you OK? Are you cold?"

She didn't say anything, again.

I took a step toward her, and at the precise moment I moved toward her, she took a step back.

"Who's there?" she said, suddenly. "I thought I saw something. Is there somebody there?"

"I'm here," I said. "Are you blind? Don't you see me?"

I took another step forward, and she took another sudden step back.

"Stay where you are," she said.

"All right," I said. "I'll stay right here."

I stayed where I was and waited.

After a moment the girl came toward me and skated around me, as if I were the center of a circle and she the circumference. Then she turned and stopped right in front of my face, and stared into my eyes.

She was looking right through me.

She didn't see me.

But she certainly sensed something.

She was absolutely aware of my presence.

"I'm here," I said. "My name is Kara. I'm right in front of you."

I wanted to reach out, to touch her, to show her that I was there, that I was real. But I didn't want to scare her away again.

"You're there, aren't you?" she said, looking right into my eyes. "You're right there."

"Yes," I said. "I'm here."

She held out a hand then. It hovered barely an inch from my face. The ice cloud of my breath in the cold air trickled through her fingers.

"Something warm," she said. "I feel warmth." She moved her hand over my face, over my head, gently sweeping over my hair, hovering there, never quite touching.

It was as if she were drawing a picture of me in the air. Tracing my outline.

Like making a figure in the snow, I thought.

"You are there," she said, with certainty. She had proved it to her own satisfaction.

"I'm here," I said.

I had been studying her, too. I'd noticed the dark pencil lines of her eyebrows. The gentle curve in her shining black hair. The dark brown of her eyes. Eyes that were looking right at me.

"Are you a ghost?" she said. "A spirit?"

"I'm real," I said, though I knew she did not hear me.

"And if you are a spirit or a specter," she said, "where are you from? And why are you here? Why have you come to us now? What is it you want to tell me?"

"I don't have anything to tell you," I said. "I don't know what I am to you. Except—maybe—a friend. Maybe you need a friend, too."

She hadn't heard me, but she answered as if she had. "You're here," she said. "That's what matters."

"I'm here," I said. "I'm a friend."

She turned and skated away from me, then circled back again in a loop. She stopped a few feet away from me.

"I need a friend right now," she said.

She hadn't heard me. She couldn't have. She was just speaking aloud. She knew only that there was some presence standing close by. She thought that presence might be a dead person of some description. She had no way of knowing whether I could hear her, or see her, or whether I meant her good or ill.

She was merely saying what she thought, what she felt, at that moment.

She looked up at the stars.

"The stars are out tonight," she said. "How beautiful they are. How cold."

"Sometimes," I said, "I'm as lonely as a star."

"I'm so lonely I'm inventing imaginary friends for myself," she said to herself with a sigh. "And so cold and tired I'm seeing things . . . Somebody's breath in the cold air . . . The lines carved by their skates in the ice."

She turned and looked right at me. "But what if you are real?" she said.

She skated over to me and stopped and peeled off her threadbare mittens and held out her hand for me to shake.

"I'm Rebecca," she said.

Rebecca.

I took my glove off.

I held out my hand.

We were about to touch, and then we didn't.

Something happened.

A dog barked in the woods.

The sound of it flew across the ice toward us, and Rebecca whipped her hand away and turned and stared at the shore, and listened.

"Dogs," she said.

There was some barking over there in the trees. Two dogs had met along one of the paths in the wild woods and were barking at each other.

"They're coming," Rebecca said. She looked at me. "You shouldn't be here. Not tonight or any other night. Whoever you are. Go!"

She turned back toward the island.

"Wait," I said. "Wait, there's nothing to be afraid of. It's just people walking their dogs."

I looked over at the shore. All I could see was the dark of the woods. I couldn't see the dogs or the people.

When I looked back, Rebecca was gone.

Sixteen

I went home the long way, by the hot dog kiosk on the other shore. Christmas lights had been strung in the trees all around and above the kiosk and it made the whole place seem kind of magical, like a grotto.

Abdul was behind the counter and we said our hellos and I ordered a vegan hot dog.

"By the way," I said to Abdul, "did you see a girl? About my age. Dark hair like me. Only hers is long. She was skating. Red skates."

He shook his head.

"She was just here," I said. "Out on the lake."

"No," Abdul said. "I saw you out there." He handed me my hot dog with squiggles of ketchup and mustard on it like waves. "But you were alone," he said.

I was alone, Abdul had said. He hadn't seen Rebecca.

I thought about that all evening. I didn't tell Mom about it. I didn't tell her about Rebecca, and I'm not sure why. I think it's because I wanted to find out what was happening for myself. Something *was* happening, something strange, and I wanted to understand it. I didn't want to be *told* about it. I wanted to *know*.

I looked up the name Rebecca on the internet. It was the only thing I knew about this strange girl, her name, and I wanted to know what it meant.

Rebecca.

It was an old Hebrew word, meaning "to join" or "to tie."

To join together, I thought. *To bind things together.*

To connect.

But it also meant "to snare."

Seventeen

Snow fell in darkness. I slept and dreamt, but I couldn't remember what I'd dreamt about when I woke.

Mom had already gone to work.

Somehow, I didn't feel so lonely today.

I was thinking about the girl I'd met on the ice last night.

I waited for it to get light. Then I put on my winter clothes and put my skates in my backpack and went out in search of Rebecca.

The snow was falling all around me.

I went down by the Viking Steps and through the newer buildings, keeping an eye out for Lars. But there was no sign of him or of any of his little gang, and I went on down into the wild woods, through the tunnel of trees.

There was no path in the woods nor any footprints. The snow falling all night long had seen to that. But I knew, roughly, where I was all the same; I knew the trees.

I stopped in the clearing where I'd seen Rebecca collecting wood for a fire and waited. I cupped my hands together around my mouth and shouted,

"Hello!"

And,

"Rebecca!"

And then, as loud as I could,

"HELLO!"

No answer.

I began to walk down to the lake, but when I got to where it usually was, it wasn't there. There was only more wood and more trees.

I must have taken a wrong turn. I turned and retraced my steps, going back over my own footprints in the snow, thinking I was sure to recognize something soon.

I knew these woods.

At least I thought I did.

Nothing looked the same.

I came to a halt.

This isn't where I am, I thought. *This is somewhere else.*

When I looked down I saw two sets of footprints on the ground: my own and another child's, and the other child's boots were the same size as mine, or so it seemed, and I couldn't tell whose were whose, or which way to go.

I went on. The trees became denser everywhere I walked. Thick clouds in the sky made it impossible to tell where the sun was, and which way was north, to the lake, and which way was south, to home.

I was lost.

I started singing. Just to hear my own voice. A voice. Anyone's voice. If you're singing, it means there's nothing wrong, and you're not lost. In a moment you'll find a path, or see a lamp post, or recognize some strange old twisted tree.

I went on through the woods.

Shortly I came to some buildings. There were three of them arranged around a courtyard, very old and European-looking, with yellow-painted walls. Wooden shutters sat closed over most of the windows, upstairs and down. The courtyard, where it peeked out from under the accumulated drifts of snow, was cobbled.

It's a farmhouse, I thought. I'd never seen it before. I didn't know it was here. I wondered if I'd stumbled on to somebody's private property.

Then I heard music.

Somebody was playing a piano.

I followed the sound of it to an open doorway and went into the farmhouse. A short dark passageway led to a larger room into which light streamed from the other side of the building. Dust hung in the air, and the room was empty, as if the people who'd lived here had moved out and the farm had been left to look after itself. Everywhere there were signs of decay: damp where the rain had gotten in, and rotten floorboards underfoot, and the smell of animals nesting somewhere inside the walls.

The sound of the piano was coming from the next room and I went through.

Rebecca was there. She had her back to me. She was sitting at a battered old upright piano in a far corner of the room, playing from memory.

I didn't say anything; I didn't want to disturb her.

She had taken her gloves off, even in this cold: her hands moved easily over the keys. The seat she was sitting on she'd made herself, it seemed, out of old bricks, stacking them one on top of the other until it was tall enough. The piano itself was out of tune and some of its keys were missing but somehow Rebecca made it work: the piece she was playing sang out into the room.

I didn't know the tune: I'd never heard it before but I knew it was beautiful. It was as if the sound filled the air around us, and I felt I was hearing it as Rebecca intended, as it was playing in her mind.

I took a step into the room, and the floorboards creaked beneath my feet.

Rebecca stopped. She turned and looked right through me.

"Hi," I said.

She didn't answer; she couldn't see me. She turned back to the piano and found her place, and played a chord that made an awful, flat sound.

She shook her head, irritated.

"Sorry," I said, though I knew she couldn't hear me.

At that moment the ground seemed to tremble.

The building seemed to shiver.

Rebecca's fingers were suspended in the air above the keys.

She was waiting for something. Listening for something.

Dust fell from the rafters and from cracks in the painted walls.

Rebecca looked at the ceiling.

An earthquake? I thought. *No.*

There was the sound of an engine, a deep powerful rumbling engine, coming closer, louder and louder, and the building began to shudder. A door creaked open on its hinges behind me. A pane of glass cracked in a window somewhere above.

Rebecca had moved quickly and slipped into a small space between the piano and the wall and had made herself very small there, as if she were hiding.

Three strings snapped inside the piano, one after another.

"Rebecca," I said, "what is it? What's happening?"

She didn't hear me: she wasn't even looking at me. She was staring at the little chair she'd made out of bricks, and I looked at it too, and the bricks trembled, and now the pile fell apart and the bricks tumbled to the floor.

At that moment the engine arrived.

A shadow swept through the rooms and I saw what it was.

It was a tank. A real tank, like the ones you see in old films, only it was bigger than they were in the films, and louder than any engine I'd ever heard. It hammered past the farmhouse on the road that pressed right up against the window, and all I could see was its wheels, and the ground shook with the force of it, and

I panicked. I thought the roof was going to fall in, and I turned and ran along the passageway and burst out through the door into the courtyard.

Glass cracked in windows above. Yellow masonry fell like paper.

I ran and slipped on wet cobblestones, and fell face-first in the snow.

Silence.

I lay there for a moment.

Cold on my face.

I opened my eyes.

I was lying in a snow drift amidst the silence of the wild woods. I listened for the rumble and tremor of the tank but there was no sound. I heard only the soft *drip-drip* of snow melting somewhere nearby.

There was no one else around.

No tank. No courtyard. No farm.

There were trees I knew; I was in the wild woods.

I lay on my back and looked up through snow-laden branches at the sky.

"Rebecca!" I called.

"Rebecca!"

All the way home I tried to work out why I could see her, but she still couldn't see me.

Eighteen

We can see them, Grandpa had said of the stars, *but they can't see us.*

We don't exist yet. We haven't been born.

Rebecca, I thought.

It's the same with Rebecca.

I could see her because I was looking back in time and space at her. But I didn't exist in her world. Not yet. I hadn't been born so she couldn't see me.

She lived in another time.

She lived in the world of the tank, that much I knew. She lived in a world where you had to hide to stay alive. She lived in a world of fear and cold.

She lived in the world of the coin I'd found in the snow.

A world of danger, and hunger, and war.

And if she lived in that world, then . . .

I had to help her.

If I was going to help her, I had to make her see me.

But how?

Maybe, I thought, *I had to reach out to her.*

Maybe we had to touch.

Maybe we had to shake hands across the universe.

That night, I watched the lake through the telescope as darkness fell.

I saw Rebecca coming along the path through the woods, collecting wood.

That was my cue. That's when I put my coat on and headed out into the cold.

I caught her trail in the wild woods. Her footprints. I followed them deeper into the trees until I saw her, up ahead, alone as ever, picking up stray bits and pieces of wood from the ground.

I stopped and watched her from behind a tree. The pockets of her overcoat were full of twigs and she had a cluster of branches under one arm. She looked a bit wild. She looked a bit like a scarecrow.

"Rebecca," I said, softly.

She didn't react.

"Rebecca," I said again, louder this time, clearly, and again she didn't react.

Then a crow took flight from a tree behind me, and Rebecca turned and looked through me and beyond me at the sky. She'd heard the crow's wings beating in the air. She hadn't heard my voice. She couldn't see me.

But I knew what I had to do.

I had to touch her.

I came out from behind the tree and walked toward her. My boots crunched in the snow and Rebecca gasped, and I stopped.

She was staring at the ground beneath my feet.

She couldn't see me.

But she could see my footprints.

She could see footprints that had just this second magically appeared in the snow. As if there were some invisible figure standing here facing her in the snow.

"Who's there?" said Rebecca. "Is somebody there?"

I took another step toward her. Another boot print materialized in the snow beneath my feet, and Rebecca's hand went to her mouth and she let go of the wood she'd been holding, and it fell to the ground at her feet.

"Stop, please," she said. "Don't come any closer, whoever you are!"

"Don't be afraid," I said. It was no use. I was stuck. I had to get to her in order to touch her, to take her hand somehow, to make her see me. But I couldn't take one more step toward her in the snow, because she would run.

Because she was scared.

I'd run too, I thought. *I'd be scared.*

Still she was looking right at me. She hadn't run. Not yet.

"I can see your breath in the air," she said.

Yes. My warm breath was fogging in the cold air; hers, too.

"You were here yesterday," she said. "On the lake."

And now she took a step toward me in the snow.

"Who are you?" she said. "How do I know I can trust you?"

I was lost for a moment. I couldn't answer her. Then I had an idea.

I sat down on my bottom in the snow.

I lay back, flat, and spread my arms as far as they would go, and I smoothed out the snow all around me.

I made a snow angel. And I knew exactly what Rebecca, watching me, would have seen: a snow angel appearing miraculously in the snow, as if it had been made by a ghost.

And do you know what Rebecca did when I was finished?

She clapped her hands. Slowly, as if I'd done something *very clever*.

"Bravo!" she said. "Bravo. So I *can* trust you. You're a friend."

I got to my feet and brushed the snow off my clothes. Then I walked toward Rebecca, slowly, and she watched the footprints appearing beneath my feet.

We stood face to face.

The breath from our lungs hung in the air in front of us.

Rebecca made the first move.

She took off her glove and held out her bare hand.

I took off my glove too and reached out and took her hand in mine.

The touch of skin.

Rebecca gasped.

"So *that's* what you look like," she said.

"You can see me?" I said.

"I can see you," she said.

"I'm Kara," I said.

She nodded.

"I'm a friend," I said. Then, "You're cold. Your hand is cold."

"Yours is warm," she said.

"Can I help you, Rebecca?" I said. "Is there anything I can do?"

She let go of my hand. There was a faint flicker of suspicion in her eye. As if she were wondering how much to give away, how much of her story to tell. As if she were wondering whose side I was on. Or perhaps she was just embarrassed.

She turned away from me. "I'm hungry," she said, and she started walking back toward the lake. "I'm hungry and I'm cold and I haven't eaten in three days."

"You're hungry?" I said, hurrying to keep up with her. I couldn't believe what I was hearing. "You haven't eaten in three days?"

"Yes," she said.

"I didn't realize," I said, "Sorry, I . . . I—"

"If you have any bread," she said. "Anything."

"Stop," I said, and she stopped.

"Come with me," I said.

I took her hand, and turned to walk down to the shore. The kiosk was open, a quarter of a mile away across the lake.

"No," said Rebecca. "No."

"Come," I said. "I'll get you some food."

She would not budge. She turned her weight against me.

"No," she said again.

I let go.

"Sorry," I said.

Rebecca nodded. "No one must see me," she said. "No one must know about me. I'm not here. Do you understand? You can't tell anybody about me."

"Are you in trouble?" I asked.

She turned away from me before she answered.

"You can't begin to imagine the trouble I'm in."

"All right," I said. "All right, I'm sorry."

Then I said, "Wait for me. I'll be back."

I went down to the shore. The lake was at its narrowest here, and I put on my skates and went out across the surface. I could see the kiosk, its pinpricks of rainbow-colored lights shining, reflected faintly in the glassy surface of the lake.

At the counter, Abdul said to me, "You again? You must like the cold and the dark."

"I need some bread," I said.

Abdul raised his eyebrows, which were bushy and still dark, even though he was old. "Bread. We don't really do bread. We do hot dogs, hamburgers. Also vegan hot dogs, vegan hamburgers."

"Just some bread," I said.

"Some bread," he said. He put a bag of hot dog rolls on the counter. "How many would you like?"

"All of it," I said.

"The whole bag?"

I nodded and went into my pocket for my money. "And some French fries—two portions. And ketchup—four packets."

My money, which was mostly coins, spilled out across the counter.

I went back quickly across the lake with the rolls and the fries in a paper bag, using the light on my phone to guide me.

There was no sign of Rebecca where I'd left her on the shore. So I skated back toward the island. I passed the figure eight she'd scored in the ice the other day.

"Rebecca!" I called.

I skated to the shore of the island.

"Rebecca!"

There was a voice then, very soft, from somewhere nearby.

"Turn out the light." It was Rebecca.

I stopped. "Why?" I said.

"Just turn it out," she said. "Please."

"All right," I said. I turned off my phone light.

Rebecca showed herself then. "Over here," she said.

She was hiding between two large old trees at the edge of the ice. She was sitting on the trunk of one of the trees, or rather, the trunk, because it was really only one tree, one enormous old tree that had grown in two different directions from the same root.

"I thought I saw someone out there," she said, looking past me at the open lake. "Someone else. On the ice."

"I didn't see anyone," I said.

I offered her the bag of food. "Here," I said.

Rebecca looked at the bag, and took it and opened it. She put her nose to the mouth of the bag and smelled. Then she reached in and pulled out a handful of fries.

She started to eat. Quickly. Ravenously.

She was as hungry as she said she was.

She was starving.

I couldn't watch. I had to look away.

Then she said, "What's this?" and I saw she'd fished out one of the ketchup packets from the bottom of the bag.

"Ketchup," I said.

She tried to open the packet but couldn't.

"Here," I said. "There's a knack to not getting it all over yourself." I took the packet from her and found the little rip at one end, and tore it open carefully.

I handed it back to her, and she tipped it up and squirted it straight into her mouth.

She closed her eyes.

Loving the ketchup.

"It really is ketchup," she sighed. "*I love ketchup.*"

She found another packet at the bottom of the bag and I opened it for her and she poured it all over her fries.

"I don't think I've seen a bottle of ketchup since before the beginning of the war," she said. "At least I don't remember seeing any since then. And I think I would remember."

Since before the beginning of the war.

I felt my blood run cold in my veins. So she was from another time.

Suddenly I remembered the farm and Rebecca playing the piano.

I remembered the tank.

Where had I been?

And when had I been there?

"Can you get more?" Rebecca said.

She was staring right at me.

"More ketchup?" I said.

"More food," she said.

"Yes," I said.

I heard a distant church clock chime somewhere out across the lake. I ought to be going home. Mom would be wondering where I was.

"Tomorrow," I said.

"Here," she said. "I'll be here. Same time."

"Yes," I said. "Same time."

"And remember," she said, "don't tell anyone about me."

I nodded.

"You give me your word," she said. She was looking right at me.

"All right," I said. "I give you my word. I won't tell anyone."

She was on her feet. She hadn't finished all the food. She took the bag with her. For later, I assumed.

"Tomorrow, then," she said. "Goodnight, Kara."

And she was gone.

I was alone.

"Goodnight, Rebecca," I whispered to the night.

Nineteen

I caught the bus out to Grandpa's house. It was an old house in the Swedish style in a village outside Stockholm. It was where they'd lived when my mother was a child. The bus took an hour, and even then I had to walk another quarter mile along an icy road.

The house had been built in the 1920s by a different family, but for my grandpa and grandma it was their first home as new parents when they bought it in the early 1970s. It was all wood on the outside, painted red, or rather red-ochre, with ornate woodwork around the doors and windows and a porch and a wooden fence built in the same style. There was a small garden out front which was sunk under the snow right now.

The trees were bare. I opened the gate and went up the path. I tapped on the front door with the metal knocker. I glanced at my watch and waited. Grandpa always said if he hadn't come to the door within two minutes I should let myself in, and sooner than that if it's cold outside.

Today I gave him a minute and then felt in my pocket for my keys. He'd given me my own key to the old house last year, and I'd treasured it, partly because it was an old key of the sort you don't see very often nowadays, but mostly because I loved the old house.

It was a thing of wonder to me, full of nooks and crannies and strange, odd spaces. When I was little it had been an inexhaustible space to explore. Now I think I had the measure of it, but I loved it nonetheless.

I unlocked the door and went in.

It was quiet. Dark, with the scent of saffron and cinnamon, leftovers from Christmas. The walls were old wood, painted and repainted over again, time after time.

Grandpa had taken down the Christmas decorations, I noticed. That was early. Twelfth Night wasn't for another couple of days yet.

"Grandpa?" I called. "Grandpa!"

There was no answer. I went through the house into the kitchen and then out the back door into the garden.

Bright sunshine on snow.

The garden went all the way down to the lake, which was frozen. At the edge of the water was a jetty, a kind of short wooden pier for smaller boats to tie up on. It extended out about five yards over the ice.

Farther along the waterfront was Grandpa's summer house. This was a much smaller house built in the same style as the bigger house: red, with ornate decorative woodworking. Grandpa had adapted it so that he could use it all year round.

I could see Grandpa's footprints in the snow going down to the summer house, but I could also see them coming back, so he wasn't there.

I went back into the main house.

"Grandpa?" I called.

This time there was an answer from somewhere high up in the house.

"Hello?"

I went to the bottom of the stairs. "It's me," I called.

"Up here," said Grandpa.

I went up—letting the wood creak as it wanted to, all the way up—past the small bedroom that had been my mother's when she was a little girl, and along the landing to where a stepladder stood, propped against the open attic hatch.

"Are you up there?" I said.

"Yes," said Grandpa, and his face appeared above me. "Come on up. But don't tell your mother."

Grandpa was decluttering. This had been forbidden by my mother. He was eighty-six years old and he lived alone, and stepladders were exactly the kind of thing Mom was thinking of when she'd forbidden him to declutter.

If he fell, there'd be no one there to pick him up. Or call an ambulance.

But since I was here, now, it would be all right. And I wasn't going to tell Mom.

I went up into the low attic space.

Light came from a small round window. The glass was as old as the house and so warped that the world outside seemed to flex and shift whenever you moved.

There was dust rising and falling in the air, and old boxes and trunks, their lids open, their contents strewn here and piled there. There were old clothes, old books, old vinyl records, and more dust, and more clothes, and an old blue winter coat so thick you could use it as a sleeping bag. I'd seen it before somewhere, in old pictures of my mother, maybe.

"Look at this," said Grandpa. "Look what I've found."

I went over to him. He undid three brown leather straps on an old, rectangular wooden box, and the lid swung back smoothly and silently, as if the little brass hinges had only very recently been oiled.

"What is it?" I said.

"Lenses," Grandpa said, pulling away a soft black cloth that had covered the contents, and there they were, rows of old astronomical lenses, each about two inches in diameter and of wildly varying thicknesses.

Grandpa took out a lens and held it up to the light.

"These are Zeiss lenses," he said. "German. This one may be a hundred years old. Although lenses never really age. It's just glass."

He handed me the lens, and I took it and held it up to my eye, like a huge monocle, and all I could see was a blur of color and light and dark.

"These were always meant to be kept with your telescope," said the light-shape that was my grandpa. "I don't know how I could have forgotten about these lenses. And mislaid them up here for so long. Now, look at me."

I took the lens monocle away from my eye.

Grandpa had placed two thick lenses over his eyes, like a pair of giant glasses. His eyes behind the lenses were so enormous he looked like an owl and I laughed, and he put the lenses back in the box.

"These are yours now," he said.

"Really?"

"Of course. You can have anything you like from up here."

"Anything?"

"Yes."

"Then I'd like that," I said, and Grandpa turned and saw what I was pointing to: the old blue winter coat.

Grandpa moved across the space and picked up the coat.

"This was your mother's when she was a teenager," he said, inspecting it. "Many afternoons and evenings in winter she was out in the cold and dark with her friends. And she was always coming home late and we were always worried about her. Always. I guess these days you can use your phone to keep in touch, wherever you are."

I nodded.

"Well, I'm sure your mother won't mind. It's a good coat. It'll keep you warm even on the coldest days." He stopped and looked me up and down. "It's a bit big for you, though, isn't it?"

"I'll grow into it," I said.

"Ah, you will, yes you will," he said, and right then a sadness passed across his face and I saw it, and then from somewhere else inside him he conjured up a smile.

"Here," he said, and he threw me the coat.

I caught it. It was heavy. It nearly knocked me over and down the hatch, but I caught it all the same.

Soup in the old dark wood kitchen downstairs for lunch. Rolls of bread with the radio on quietly in the background. Grandpa and I didn't speak, just ate.

There was a knot in the grain of the wood on the kitchen table and I found myself staring at it while I ate. It looked a bit like an island surrounded by a river of wood, and I thought of Rebecca.

The old blue winter coat sat on the seat next to me. I was glad of it. I knew exactly what I was going to do with it.

Afterward, I washed up, by hand, while Grandpa dried and put everything away. Then he looked at his watch, and turned the radio off and boiled the kettle on the old gas stove.

I went to the window. The sky was clear; the sun was low.

Grandpa filled a flask with coffee and we went out without a word into the garden and across the snow to the summer house.

We went up the steep wooden flight of stairs to the top room of the summer house. It was airy up there, south-facing, with an enormous window and a big wide-open view of the frozen lake.

There was also a telescope in there, much bigger than the one that had been handed down to me. Grandpa had even put a new window into the roof so that he could point the telescope through it.

He poured himself a cup of coffee from his flask and sipped it slowly while we waited for it to get dark. I'd brought an apple with me from the kitchen but I let it sit in my pocket, saving it for later.

We didn't talk.

I realized in the silence that there were things we needed to talk about.

There was Grandpa's health, and he couldn't talk about that.

There was Rebecca, and I couldn't talk about that.

But we could talk about the past.

I asked him about the war, the Second World War, and what he remembered.

"I was a child," Grandpa said. "We lived in Malmö then, in the south of Sweden. Denmark had been overrun by the Nazis. Norway, too. But Copenhagen was only a few miles across the water from where we lived, and I could see, you understand? I could see the war. I watched it with the telescope, the one you have now."

He paused to take a sip of his coffee. I took a bite of my apple.

I was sitting on a cushion on the floor.

The dark had come quickly. It was already dark enough to see the stars.

Grandpa put his cup of coffee down on the small table under the window and put his eye to the telescope's viewfinder.

"I saw firefights over Denmark," he continued. "British and German planes attacking each other. I saw fighter-bombers explode in midair. I saw flames falling on the surface of the sea."

"Were we neutral? In the war?" I asked.

"We, as in Sweden?"

"Yes."

"We were neutral," he said.

He turned away from the telescope and tapped me on the shoulder in the dark.

"Your turn," he said. "Look."

I looked through the telescope.

I saw the planet Mars, half in light, half in dark.

"Mars," I said.

"Yes," he said. "The Bringer of War."

He picked up his cup of coffee again.

"Back then," he said, "we were afraid. We were strong, but we thought we were weak. So we didn't intervene. We gave help to both sides, I think. Information, supplies . . . Iron."

I looked at him across the darkening room.

"But the Jews," I said. "Everything that happened to them. Everything that was done to them."

It felt important, right then, to say the words.

"They were murdered," I said.

"Yes," said Grandpa. "They were murdered. And the rest. Anyone who didn't fit in. Anyone who might cause trouble. Anyone they were afraid of."

He paused, thinking about what he was going to say.

"We let the world down," he said. "We were stronger than we thought we were. We would not have been overrun. We would have dug in. We would have fought like Vikings."

His eyes shone in the darkness.

"One thing I do know," he said.

"What's that?" I said.

"Your generation won't let the world down."

Twenty

That night I took the elevator down to the lobby. I had my skates with me. I was wrapped up against the cold. The big blue coat Grandpa had given me was stuffed into my backpack: I was going to give it to Rebecca; she needed it.

I came out of the elevator and crossed the lobby and went straight out into the cold air.

Then I stopped dead.

Lars was there.

Lars, who I'd hit in the face with a snowball. He hadn't forgotten about me.

He was sitting on a bench a few feet away with three other boys, the boys who'd ambushed me in the snowball fight. They were smoking electronic cigarettes. Little clouds wafted up. Little pinpricks of light glowed.

There was a moment as I stood there, a brief moment, when Lars hadn't seen me. I could have made a run for it. Probably I had enough of a head start to get away, down the Viking Steps, before he'd even seen it was me.

But I froze.

It's one of the things fear can do to you.

I froze, and right then Lars looked over through a cloud of smoke and saw me. He frowned. He recognized me. He remembered the snowball smacking him in the face.

He got to his feet and walked toward me.

"Where do you think you're going?" he said.

I didn't answer.

He came closer.

I backed away.

Lars ducked down and grabbed a handful of snow off the ground, and kept coming toward me, packing the snow tight in his hands into a cold hard ball.

I kept backing away.

Behind him the other boys were on their feet, watching. One of them scooped up some snow, too.

"Hey," said Lars. "I'm talking to you. Where do you think you're—"

I didn't hear him say *going* because I'd gone.

I turned and made a run for it back to the lobby.

Behind me, Lars threw the snowball. It sailed past me and smacked into the glass of the lobby door. Then I was at the door myself, and I tore off the glove on my right hand and punched in the four-digit door code as fast as I could.

The code was 1392.

I heard running behind me.

There was a click, and a tiny red light came on above the number panel. I pushed the door open and went through it and closed it behind me, just as Lars arrived, slamming up against the glass.

The door shuddered. But the glass held.

I looked at him through the glass.

"What's the code for the door?" he said. His voice was muted, muffled by the glass. "Hey, you. I'm talking to you. Tell me the code."

The other boys came and joined him at the door. They pressed up against the glass, pulling faces, jeering at me, making rude hand signals while the glass misted up with their hot breath around them.

I shook my head.

I turned and walked back to the elevator. I pressed the button to call it and heard the dull rattle of the machinery inside as it began its descent, high above.

Lars rapped on the glass of the door with his bare knuckles.

"Hey, let me in," he said. "I just want to talk to you."

I ignored him. I kept telling myself I was safe in here.

I kept my eyes straight ahead.

But Lars kept rapping on the glass.

"Hey! Hey, you! You might as well let me in. I know people who live here. I can get the code for the door anytime I like. I can get in . . ."

I made a mistake then.

I looked back.

I looked back at Lars, and he put his tongue out and licked the glass, leaving a disgusting smear all along it.

The elevator arrived finally and I stepped inside.

All the way up all I could hear was the laughter of his little gang ringing in my ears.

I went back to my room. I looked through the telescope but what I saw seemed blurred and foggy and when I tried to focus I realized that my hand was shaking.

I was so angry and ashamed.

I wanted to hurt Lars.

If you had given me a button to press right then that would have made Lars and his puny little gang vanish into thin air, and nobody would ever have heard from them again, I would have gladly pressed it.

I was thankful they didn't make such buttons.

I sat down on the bed and took deep breaths.

I realized that what had just happened would stick in my thoughts for a while, that whenever my mind wandered, that's what would come into it: the image of it, Lars licking the glass.

Part of me realized that was what he wanted. To get inside my head. That's what all bullies want.

Then I thought of something else.

I thought of Rebecca.

Help Rebecca, I said to myself.

That's your task. Forget about Lars.

I went back to the telescope and turned the focus wheel carefully until I could see the island, and I zeroed in on the darker trees there.

There was the very faint low red glow of a fire.

"I'm sorry I couldn't make it tonight," I said, though I knew there was no way she could hear me. No way for me to get a message to her.

Somehow I didn't think she had a cell phone. I didn't think she knew what one was.

Twenty-one

The sun was bright on the snow and the ice.

I was on the lake early.

I went out to the island.

When I came to it, by daylight, I saw that it was much bigger than it seemed before.

It was a hundred yards wide and long. The shore in normal times would have been swampy and mulchy. Now it was frozen mush. Craggy branches twisted and turned this way and that, dipping in and out of the darkly frozen surface like the curving bodies of diving sea monsters.

The trees were old and big and wet with lichens. So old, some of them, that they hung out over the water. In places the trunks appeared to be cut through by the ice.

I went ashore.

The bare trees rapidly gave way to stands of evergreen pine in the interior of the island. This was what made the island a good place for things to grow. The pines clung on, even in winter, and held the fertile earth in place, providing some shelter from the worst of the winds.

It was also what made the island a good place to hide.

"Rebecca?" I called.

"Rebecca!"

I came to the remains of a fire near the heart of the island. White ash, wet through, lay in the middle of a dark circle where the snow had completely melted away.

I dug down into the pile of ashes with the toe of my boot, looking for embers, but it was out. It looked like it had been out for some time.

Nearby stood a bivouac, a simple handmade shelter. Cut branches had been leaned against a low tree branch to form a triangular hide. The roof had been covered with moss.

I went inside. It was as cold inside as out, but at least it was dry. It was empty but for an old checked blanket.

I opened my backpack. I took out the blue coat and left it, folded, in the bivouac. Then from my pockets I brought out a stash of food I'd brought for Rebecca: apples and bananas, cookies, cartons of fruit drink, some yogurts. I picked up the blanket, thinking I could hide the food underneath it, and that's when I found the notebook.

It was a child's workbook, like the ones we used to have at school, but it was old and worn, and there was no name on the cover. It had been wrapped in the blanket, and as I lifted it up the notebook fell to the ground in front of me.

I picked it up and turned the pages. Inside, there were careful charcoal drawings of the island and the lake and the bivouac. There were drawings of birds in the sky and of clouds and the stars. There was a drawing of a plane in the sky, high up, as if the person who was drawing it were lying flat on the ground looking up.

It was an old plane. It looked like something out of a war film.

I turned the page, and I came to the map.

Rebecca had drawn a map of the lake in pencil. It was very detailed and ran over several pages, showing the island, and the woods on the shore where she collected the firewood, and the long twisting and turning shoreline of the great lake as it ran west, farther and farther inland, into the heart of the country.

She had made some strange marks on the surface of the lake—arrows and exclamation marks and areas of cross-hatched shading—and I couldn't see what they were for or what they were supposed to mean.

Currents in the water?

Places where it was good to fish?

I had no idea.

I was getting cold; I'd been sitting still for too long, staring at the pictures in the notebook. I put it away under the blanket and hid the food there too, and after one last look around to make sure there was no sign of Rebecca, I went home.

Twenty-two

At home, I made dinner. But my mind was elsewhere, out there on the lake. So I undercooked the peas and overcooked the macaroni and I burned my finger on the side of the pot when I poured the pasta water into the sink.

I needed to talk to Mom.

I brought the food to the table and Mom closed her laptop.

"Thanks," she said.

"We're out of tea lights," I said. "And candles."

"Don't worry," she said, and then added, "we're the light."

Meaning *Lukas*, our family name.

It was something she used to say to me when I was younger and afraid of the dark, after she'd put the light out in my room.

You're the light. So you don't have to be afraid of the dark.

The meal was not so horrible in the end, and when we'd finished, I said, "I need some advice."

Mom nodded. "I thought something was up. What is it? What's troubling you?"

I wasn't sure how to begin.

"I have a friend," I said.

Mom waited.

"I think she's in trouble," I said.

"Go on," Mom said.

"I don't think things are working out for her at home right now. I don't think she gets enough to eat," I said.

"Who is it?" Mom asked. "Someone I know?"

"No."

"Is it someone at school?"

"No," I said. "I can't tell you who it is."

Mom leaned forward and took my hand. "Kara, who is it?"

"She asked me not to tell anybody about her," I said.

"Kara," Mom said. "Tell me."

I can't. I won't.

"I gave my word," I said.

Mom nodded and let go of my hand.

"I'm sorry," I said. "I just can't tell you who it is."

Mom nodded again. She was intrigued, interested, a little worried. I could see her mind was racing. She was looking for a workaround. How to find out more about this girl. How to get around a promise between two friends.

There's always a workaround, she says. There's always another way.

"All right," she said. "I understand. It's a promise. But I want you to promise me something, too."

"What?"

"Here's what you're going to do. You're going to stay close to this mystery girl, OK? You keep talking to her. You make sure she knows she's not alone. You make sure she knows she's got a friend in you. That she's got someone she can rely on. Then, you bring her here if you can, so I can meet her, so we can feed her and talk to her. Are you with me?"

"Yes."

"OK. Now, I don't know what kind of trouble this girl is in, but this is what I want you to promise me, OK?"

"Yes."

"Promise me you'll persuade her to talk to an adult and ask for help. That's it. That's all. If you do nothing else. If you can't get her to come here. Just persuade her to talk to an adult. It doesn't have to be a parent. It can be anybody. A teacher at school. Someone in the church. Just someone she trusts. Because there's always someone you can reach out and talk to. Even when you think you're alone. Even when you think you'll get in trouble for speaking up, which she won't, I promise you. Because there's always an adult, somewhere nearby, who'll understand what's going on and who'll help."

Always. Trust me.

"Are you with me?" Mom asked. "Will you tell her?"

"Yes," I said.

I promise.

"Do you need money?" Mom asked.

"Maybe," I said. I didn't think it could hurt.

"I'll put some into your account," said Mom, and she reached for her phone. "Buy Mystery Girl some lunch. Take her to McDonald's. Whatever she wants."

You should know by now, if you don't already, that my Mom is amazing.

Twenty-three

In my room I scanned the lake until I found Rebecca. Then I went straight down to the lobby and peered out through the glass in the door.

There was no Lars.

The coast was clear.

I went out. But I didn't go down to the lake right away. I took a bus back across the bridge and let it carry me down to the road on the north side of the lake. I got off by the kiosk where I usually met Grandpa.

Abdul was there and I bought more fries and ketchup from him. Then I strapped on my skates and set out across the lake.

There was a fire burning in the clearing on the island. I could smell it before I could see it. The air was cold and still and the smoke drifted out over the lake.

I went quickly from the shore through the trees to the stand of pine. I saw the fire glowing red as I approached.

"Rebecca?"

The fire crackled and I heard movement.

"Rebecca?"

I looked at the bivouac.

There was someone in there. But it wasn't Rebecca.

I went closer.

Someone was cowering away from me, trying to hide behind the blanket in the farthest corner.

"Hey," I said. "Hey there. Don't be afraid."

I came closer.

"Hey," I said again. "I brought bread. I'm a friend."

I waited.

A face came forward into the light.

It was a boy. He was about eight years old with very dark hair and pale skin. He was terrified of me. And he was wearing the old blue coat I'd left for Rebecca even though it was about three sizes too big for him.

"Don't be afraid," I said.

I knelt on the ground in front of the bivouac. Not too close, but close enough to see him, and for him to see me. I put the paper bag of food on the ground between us.

It was an offering.

"Here," I said. "Fries. And ketchup."

The boy nodded.

"I'm Kara," I said. "Who are you?"

"Samuel," said the boy.

Samuel, I thought.

She has a brother, I thought.

"You're Rebecca's brother," I said.

"Yes," he said.

He was intense. There was a strange energy around him. It was as if every word had to be wrenched out of him, like speaking was a series of controlled explosions.

He nodded, strangely, as if he'd read my thoughts, and then he came forward and opened the bag of fries and started to eat.

I wondered why I'd never seen him out on the lake.

"Can you skate?" I said. "Do you need skates? I can bring some."

He just looked at me.

"Are you in trouble?" I asked. "Are you and Rebecca in some kind of trouble? Is somebody after you?"

He didn't answer, but I felt he had. Oddly I felt that the answer to the questions I'd asked him was *Yes.*

Yes, we are in trouble.

Yes, somebody is after us.

"Are you in danger?" I asked.

Yes, came the thought.

"Am I in danger?" I asked.

Yes.

Samuel continued to eat his fries, staring at me.

"This lake goes on for miles and miles," I said. "It goes all the way into the heart of the country. You and Rebecca could skate away, far away, and nobody would ever find you."

"I don't skate," said Samuel, finally.

"Well, it's easy," I said. "I can teach you. It'll be fun. I could teach you in a day, maybe."

There was a sound then, behind, and I turned, and there was Rebecca coming with more wood for the fire.

"He doesn't skate," she said.

"Why not?" I said.

"He can't."

I wasn't quite sure what that meant.

She put more wood on the fire. It hissed wetly.

"What do you mean?" I said.

She looked at me. "He can't walk. Let alone skate."

There was a silence amongst us then. I didn't know what to say. Samuel watched me darkly, eating his fries. Finally I said, "I brought more food."

"Thank you," said Rebecca. "And hello, and welcome."

She gave me a hug.

"This is where you live," I said.

"For now," she said.

"Are you homeless?" I said.

"For now," she said, sitting down. She dug into the remains of the fries and found the ketchup packets and squirted them over everything and ate quickly.

"The food is appreciated," she said. "We've been so hungry. I've been so stupid. I lost what money we had—the last of it—somewhere in the snow. It must have fallen out of my pocket while I was playing childish games."

The coin—the German coin—was *hers*.

"I-I-I didn't realize," I stammered, but before I could say any more Samuel had pulled out the bag of hot dog rolls I'd brought and taken one out.

"He has a question," said Rebecca.

Samuel nodded. "Do you eat dogs?"

"Dogs?" I said.

"Yes," said Samuel.

Hot dogs.

"No," I said. "The rolls—the bread—they're for sausages."

"Ah," said Rebecca.

"They're called hot dogs," I said. "But they're just sausages. Pig, mostly. Pork. I don't eat them myself. I'm vegetarian. Vegan, mostly."

Rebecca nodded. "We don't eat pork," she said.

The fries were gone. Rebecca found the last packet of ketchup and squirted it on Samuel's bread. Then she peeled the entire packet open, carefully, and proceeded to lick it clean. When she was finished she said, "Where do you get this food?"

"At the kiosk," I said. "On the shore."

Rebecca looked at me like she had no clue what I was talking about.

I raised my arm and pointed back over my shoulder.

"It's not far," I said. "You can see it."

Rebecca nodded and got to her feet.

"Show me," she said.

Twenty-four

We went out on the ice, Rebecca and I, leaving Samuel on the island. We skated across the lake until I saw the kiosk, a little rainbow pinprick of light in the distance.

"There," I said. "Look."

"Where?" said Rebecca.

"There," I said again. "Where I'm pointing. Follow my arm."

Rebecca aligned herself with my arm and looked.

"I don't see it," she said flatly. "I don't see anything."

"What do you see?" I said.

"Nothing," she said. "No light anywhere. Bare trees. Darkness along the shore."

I didn't understand it.

I couldn't understand it.

And then Rebecca showed me.

She grabbed my hand. She had taken off her glove and now she took hold of my wrist. Her fingers found the thin circle of bare skin between my glove and the sleeve of my warm winter coat.

And then I saw what she saw.

Darkness fell like a stone dropped by a bird.

What I saw was another lake, another shore. Frozen, yes, surrounded by trees, yes, but it was not Mälaren. It was not my lake. We were somewhere else, somewhere far away, somewhere darker.

"Do you see?" she said.

"Yes," I said.

I stared out into the darkness of Rebecca's world, and I realized something.

I'd seen this before. I'd been here before.

I remembered the power cut a few days ago. Grandpa had called to tell me about the meteor shower that was coming. I looked through the telescope. Then came the power cut. The lights went out all over the city, the skyglow faded and I could see the stars.

Except there hadn't been any power cut.

The power had stayed on all the time.

I'd been looking in a different place. I'd been looking into Rebecca's world. No city lights burned there because there was no city where Rebecca lived. There were no electric lights of any kind for miles, and on a clear night you could always see the stars.

I had already been here.

I had already seen this world.

Rebecca let go of my wrist.

"What do you see?" she said. "Something else?"

"Yes," I said.

She nodded. "Show me," she said.

She rolled up her sleeve. I took off my glove and grabbed her wrist and held it. I felt how cold her skin was, and Rebecca gasped.

She saw the kiosk, far away, and farther away, the lights in the windows of the tower buildings, and the strings of street lights along both shores, and the nightglow of the city projected up on to the clouds.

"Do you see?" I said.

"I see," she said. She seemed breathless, almost as if she were going to faint. Then she said, and it was as if she were pleading with me, "Let me go . . . Let me go . . ."

I let her go.

She seemed to relax then. Her breath came back.

"We're in different places," she said, "you and I."

"Different times," I whispered.

She shook her head at that. "Different worlds."

I remembered the coin.

"I found a coin," I said. "In the snow. It had an eagle on it. And a swastika."

"A five-pfennig piece?" she said.

"Yes. It's yours, I think. It must be. You lost it."

"Do you have it?" she said.

"I don't have it with me," I said, "but I can get it back . . . I will get it back. Tomorrow."

Rebecca nodded. "The coin is death," she said. "Death to people like me. But it still buys food. There are still farms here that will sell to us."

"And where is here?" I said.

"Here is here," she said, turning toward me. "You and me."

"But where are we?" I said. "Where are we now?"

She hesitated, and for a moment I thought she wasn't going to answer me, and then she said the name of a place I didn't recognize.

"Where's that?" I said, and then Rebecca told me where she lived.

It wasn't Sweden; Rebecca had never been to Sweden. She grew up in another country, hundreds of miles away across the sea. She was still there.

We were in two different places, at two different times. Somehow we'd met across this gulf of space and time: she was still stuck there, and it came to me that I was the only person who could help her.

"OK," I said. I didn't know what else to say, and Rebecca didn't ask me where I was—where *here* was for me. Perhaps she already knew. Perhaps she couldn't quite believe it.

There was a sound like a gun being fired in the distance. We turned and looked in the same direction: toward the eastern end of the lake.

I was not sure what I'd heard or what I was seeing. It looked like a firework shooting up in the sky.

"What is it?" I said.

Rebecca didn't answer. The firework bloomed into a bright, falling star, glittering yellow. It was spectacular in its own way, falling through the air.

"It's a flare," said Rebecca.

The ice glowed yellow as the star came down. I could see for a mile or more in every direction.

Which meant we could also be seen.

"They're looking for us," said Rebecca.

The flare landed on the ice a few hundred feet away. It continued to burn, out there, smoldering, spitting little nuggets of yellow light intermittently.

"They're coming," said Rebecca. "We must go. Come on!"

"Who's coming?" I said. "I don't see anybody."

Somebody blew a whistle, faintly, far away. Rebecca was no longer standing beside me.

She'd gone. She was skating away.

I heard dogs barking, somewhere out there in the gloom at the eastern end of the lake. I couldn't see any farther than where the flare lay sputtering on the ice.

There was the sound of a pack of dogs running over the surface of the frozen lake. It was a low kind of sound, a drumming, and above it the dogs could be heard yelping and barking and snarling.

They appeared, all at once, in the dull yellow oval of light cast by the stranded flare.

A dozen black dogs: hunting dogs. Dobermanns.

I opened my mouth to scream but nothing came out of it in the cold air. The dogs were shapeshifting silhouettes against the fading yellow flare. They grew bigger with every passing moment. Then the flare behind them burned out, and they came on in near darkness.

I was stuck to the spot. I could not think. I could not run. I remained there, in the darkness.

Sounds of paws and dog claws on the ice and barking.

Moonlight on glistening slick black fur.

They were upon me. I still could not move. I kicked inside at my own legs, willing them to budge. But there I remained, and the dogs had caught me.

I screamed. "Nooooooooooo!"

And they ran straight through me.

Like ghosts.

Like projections on a movie screen.

Like I wasn't in their world.

They passed through me and as they did they began, rapidly, to fade, disappearing into the air even as they went on, charging toward some other prey.

They hadn't seen me at all. They weren't hunting me. They were hunting someone else. They were hunting Rebecca.

I watched them fade away to nothing.

Only then did I remember to breathe.

* * * /// * * *

Twenty-five

Rebecca and Samuel were Jews. They were in hiding. The year was 1944.

They were in hiding because the leaders and the people of the country in which they lived were trying to kill them. The Nazis had already taken away every other member of their family. They had taken them to the work camps. They had taken them to the extermination camps.

All of this happened because they were Jews.

Trucks came to their house in the country. Soldiers rounded everybody up. Rebecca and Samuel survived because they were playing hide-and-seek in the cellar.

The trucks departed. Upstairs, only the cook and the housekeeper, who were not Jews, remained. They, along with Rebecca and Samuel's parents, had pretended the children had gone to Sweden two weeks previously to visit their aunt.

Now the cook and the housekeeper told Rebecca and Samuel to go for real.

"Take what you want but travel light," said the housekeeper, who loved Samuel. "We cannot hide you here. Soldiers will come back to loot the house. Everything that is yours will be taken and the house will be given to the wife of an officer in the Gestapo."

Then the cook said, "They'll kill us if they find you here when they come back."

So Rebecca pried the mezuzah from the wood of the door and kissed it and they left that day.

They had a bicycle. Samuel clung to Rebecca.

They came to the island.

This is a hiding place, thought Rebecca. They could stay here and wait out the war.

Germany was losing. It would not be long.

Then came the winter. The last winter of the war. The lake froze around the island.

Strange things began to happen. They became aware of another world, a hidden world, rubbing up against their own. Samuel heard ghostly voices in the night but could not make out what they were saying. By day, Rebecca saw spectral figures skating on the lake. She ignored them.

She assumed it was the starvation.

They were slowly losing their minds.

Then one night the sky was criss-crossed with meteor showers. Rebecca heard a girl singing in the woods but couldn't find her anywhere. Footprints that were not her own appeared in the snow, vanished, and reappeared again.

Time seemed to be repeating itself. The geography of the lake changed: it could not be relied upon. Only the island was the same, all the time.

Perhaps the island is a door, thought Rebecca.

A gateway to another time, another place.

But if it's a door, why can't I go through it?

Because it's locked, she thought. *Locked on the other side. And until I can find someone who can open it, it's useless to me.*

Stay alive, she thought.

Fetch wood.

Keep warm.

Find food.

They just had to make it through the winter.

Twenty-six

I went back to the antique shop in the Old Town. I had to get the five-pfennig coin back for Rebecca.

I had the receipt with me. I took it out as I turned the corner from the docks and walked up the cobbled street toward the shop.

There was a CLOSED sign in the window.

I looked at my watch. It was past ten in the morning, and a weekday. The shop should have been open.

I peered in through the glass of the door. The lights were off. The interior looked ghostly. A single splinter of light shone up from the door at the bottom of the steps behind the counter. There was nobody around that I could see.

I knocked on the glass. Then I noticed an old doorbell button set into the wall by the side of the door. I pressed it and thought I heard a faint, faraway buzz.

I pressed the buzzer again, looking through the glass.

I was so angry with myself for giving Rebecca's coin away, I'd become determined to get it back. I pressed the buzzer again and held it there, listening to the distant, frantic sound, and then I saw what I'd missed: there was a small handwritten note placed low down in the glass of the front door.

"Closed due to a death in the family," it said.

I took my finger off the buzzer and stared at the note. I wondered who had died. Probably it was the old man I'd met the other day, Albert.

I wondered how I'd get Rebecca's coin back.

I wondered what would happen to the dog.

Right then, there was a sound from inside the shop: a long, discordant chiming. The old clocks that lined the walls inside were marking the hour, and I listened to the strange metallic sound until it faded away.

It started to rain and I turned for home.

Coin or no coin, Rebecca and Samuel had to eat.

I went out to the island in the early afternoon and left a loaf of bread and two apples and a carton of juice in the bivouac. Then I went home and waited for night to fall.

Twenty-seven

Come darkness, I took the elevator down to the lobby.

I had my ski poles with me, and my toboggan. It was a sturdy blue plastic one with a long guide rope. It was almost as tall as me. I hadn't used it at all so far this winter, but I had an idea it was going to be useful.

I'd been thinking about Samuel. I'd been thinking about how I could help him.

In the lobby I came right up to the glass in the door and looked out to make sure there was nobody lying in wait for me. I was half-expecting—half-dreading—seeing Lars outside with his little gang. But there was no one there. Perhaps it was too cold.

I went out into the night with the toboggan. Down the Viking Steps and past the newer apartment buildings. Then I was in the wild woods and I could pull the toboggan along behind me in the snow.

I came to the shore, put my skates on, and tied the guide rope around my waist. I went out on the lake, poling the ice, pulling the toboggan.

I came to the island and unclipped my skates. I parked the toboggan upright in a wedge of snow between two trees. Then I walked through the trees to the camp. The fire was almost out. Rebecca and Samuel were there, sleeping, in the bivouac.

I didn't want to wake them. I wondered how exhausting their lives must be. To be always afraid, always on the lookout for danger. I thought sleep must be a relief. If you could sleep in this cold.

It was better to leave them in peace.

I began to make up the fire as best I could. A pile of branches and twigs sat nearby drying slowly in the warmth of the fire. I picked the ones that were the least wet and laid them carefully over the hot ashes. The trick is to place the wood at the hottest place of the fire where the heat rises. So you pile them around this point making a kind of pointed cone, and the flames from underneath will eventually catch them. You just have to wait.

I waited. First came some white smoke that made me choke. Then the smoke cleared, and blue and yellow flames leapt up around the fresh wood.

I stayed there, looking into the flames. I don't know how long I remained like that, unmoving, eyes wide open. I know I felt safe, and warm and comfortable. I know I felt like I was watching over Rebecca and Samuel, guarding them.

Somebody said my name.

I looked over and saw that Rebecca was awake, lying on her side in the bivouac, her body curled around Samuel's under the blanket, her eyes open.

"Rebecca," I said.

"You brought food," she said, sitting up.

"I did," I said.

"Thank you. We've eaten it already."

"That's what it was for," I said.

"Don't you need it for yourself?" she said. "For your family?"

"I have enough," I said. "We have enough. My mother and I. Too much, really."

"Are you rich?" Rebecca asked.

It was hard to explain. Mom and I weren't rich. We had a monthly budget we had to stick to, and Stockholm is a very expensive city to rent an apartment in. That was one of the reasons Mom had to work such long hours. But we were rich compared to Rebecca and Samuel. We had more than enough to eat. We had a roof over our heads. Our apartment was warm in winter and cool in summer.

Rebecca and Samuel had precisely nothing in the world.

Except, they had each other.

And they had me.

"I'm not rich," I said. "But I have enough to share with you and Samuel."

Rebecca nodded. She seemed satisfied by this answer. She got up and came to sit beside me by the fire.

"I brought something else," I said. "For Samuel."

"What?" said Rebecca.

"What? What did you bring?" said Samuel, sitting up.

He had heard his name in his sleep. Now he was awake.

We were on the lake. Rebecca skated alongside me. I pulled the toboggan, fast, and in the back of the toboggan sat Samuel, wrapped up under a blanket.

He was smiling. Actually, really smiling.

Grinning from ear to ear.

Loving the speed. Loving the motion.

I pulled, faster and faster.

Then I changed direction suddenly, turning against my own momentum, and the toboggan swung out in a great wide circle behind me and I heard Samuel screaming, "Wheeeee!"

Rebecca took over and I skated behind them, and she pulled him faster even than I could pull him because she was older than me and bigger than me, and her muscles were stronger than mine because they had to be, because of everything she had to do, every day, just to stay alive.

Samuel spun and circled and flew on the ice until we were too tired to pull him any more, and we came in breathless to the island shore.

Rebecca lifted Samuel out of the toboggan and carried him back through the trees to the bivouac.

I went across the lake to get fries and ketchup from Abdul's kiosk.

I came back across the ice with the food using the light on my phone to guide me until I was sure I could see the dark outline of the island ahead. Then, as Rebecca had told me to do, I turned off the light, and went on in near darkness.

I nearly tripped over Rebecca as I approached the island.

She was lying down on the ice. On her front, with her cheek and her ear to the ice.

I stopped. "Rebecca?" I said.

"*Sssh,*" she whispered.

I waited and watched her. After a moment she opened her eyes.

"What are you doing?" I said.

"I'm listening to the ice," she said. "I'm listening to its secret sound . . . to its song."

"What does it say?" I asked.

"It says . . . just a minute. Yes. It says, 'Kara Lukas asks too many questions'."

She laughed and bounced up to her feet.

"Seriously," I said. "What does it say?"

"It tells me where it's weak and where it's strong," she said, and she turned and looked out past the island to the west, at the lake stretching away into the gray distance, and she continued, "It tells me where it's safe to walk and where the ice will break."

Then she looked at me.

"I've been making a map," she said. "I've been marking it up where the ice is too thin for us to walk."

The map.

So that's what it was for.

Of course.

Rebecca looked at the bags of fries I was holding. "Did you bring ketchup?"

Samuel was asleep as soon as he'd eaten and climbed back under the blanket.

Rebecca and I sat by the glowing fire.

"This has been a good day," Rebecca said. "We can still have good days."

A silence hung in the air and we stared at the fire.

It crackled.

"The coin I found," I said. "Your coin. It had a date on it. A year."

Rebecca nodded.

"Nineteen forty-two," I said.

Rebecca smiled at me. Then she said, "What year do you think it is?"

"I don't know," I said. "I don't know where I am when I'm with you and Samuel."

I stared at the fire.

"All I know," I said, "is you're very far from home."

Rebecca nodded sadly to herself. Then she spoke again.

"We're lost, Kara. Samuel and I just got a little lost in time looking for a safe place, for somewhere to hide. The island—" she said, and broke off and laughed.

She took a deep breath and went on. "The island . . . the island was a good place to hide in the summer. No one came here. No one knew we were here. No one could get out to the island. We slept by day and picked berries. By night I'd hide in the trees on the shore and try to catch fish. This is where we were going to stay. We were going to sit here, and sleep here and dream, and wait for the war to end."

"Then the winter," I said.

"Yes," she said. "The lake turned to ice. Which means anybody can walk across the ice. Anybody can find us. Dogs can track us across the ice. It's a bridge between the island and the land, between the island and the universe. Everything is connected once again."

"If you can make it through this winter," I said, "if you can hang on until the ice melts, you'll be safe again."

"Maybe," she said. "Maybe not. You've seen the dogs. They know we're here. I found shell casings in the snow on the shore. I think they've left men with rifles on the shore. Snipers."

"You're safe now," I said. "Right now. Tonight."

Rebecca nodded. She looked at me then, her eyes locked on mine above the fire, and said, "I feel safe when you're here, Kara. For some reason I don't understand. I don't know why that is.

Maybe it's the courage you bring. Maybe it's because you found us, somehow, and you're a good person. I believe in you, and if there are good people in the world, then we may make it."

"What's going to happen?" I asked.

Rebecca looked up at the sky, at the stars.

"There's a plane coming," she said. "British, I think. It's going to stall up there, above the lake, and they're going to have to land on the ice. But if we can get to them before they've fixed the problem with their engines, maybe there's room for Samuel and me. Maybe we can go to England."

I felt that I was on the verge of understanding something vital. But the verge was a cliff edge, a precipice with darkness beyond it, and I did not want to go down there. It was something about Rebecca, about what she knew, and how she knew, and when she lived, and when she died.

Despite myself, I asked the question that had been forming on my lips.

"How do you know about the plane?" I said. "How do you know it's going to stall?"

"Because I know," she said. "I saw it."

She looked at me across the fire.

Tears shone in her eyes.

"Because I slipped on the ice," she said.

Twenty-eight

Rebecca slipped on the ice. She fell. She hurt her back. She lay there, winded, trying to get her breath back.

She felt warm. Which was odd. It was the coldest night of the year so far. She was lying on her back on a frozen lake looking up at the stars in the clear night sky, and she felt warm.

How peculiar.

She tried to name the stars she could see. She tried to remember their names. But something was missing. She was getting weaker and weaker and weaker.

She tried to remember how long she'd been out on the ice today. Four hours? Three hours? Every hour was an hour away from the fire. Every hour was an hour away from the shared warmth of the blanket and the bivouac. She wondered if she was dying of hypothermia out here on the ice.

She couldn't move anyway. She wasn't strong enough to move. So she looked up and wished upon a star. She picked one, more or less at random, and made a wish.

Then she heard a plane. It was coming in low over the lake. The engine stalled, right up there in the sky over Rebecca.

It was British plane, Rebecca knew. A reconnaissance plane, Samuel said later when she'd described it to him because he knew about these things.

Still, one of its engines was out. Blown. The wind was whistling over its wings.

It came in low, gliding freely, and Rebecca realized they were going to try to land on the lake, using the ice as a runway. What choice did they have?

She laughed.

Then she crossed her fingers and hoped and hoped.

"I waited for the explosion," Rebecca said. "I lay there and I listened for the sound of the crash. But none came. They'd done it. They'd landed the plane on the ice.

"Later, I heard the plane taking off again. They'd fixed her up . . . they were going home.

"I tried to get up. But I couldn't do it, I couldn't move, and I felt warm all over . . ."

Then, she said, she saw a light.

A candle.

She turned her head until her cheek rested against the ice. She looked to the west and saw a wooden jetty there, protruding out over the ice. Two young people, children possibly, were sitting right on the end of the jetty. One of the children held a single burning candle while the other sheltered it, keeping it alight.

"Their faces," Rebecca said, "seemed blurry. Smudged. One of them was a girl with dark hair. The other was a boy, a little older than the girl, with short blond hair.

"Two children on a little wooden jetty with a candle in the darkness. That was all I could see. But I felt hope. I felt my heart lift.

"And then," she said, "the candle went out.

"I woke in darkness," Rebecca said. "In the absolute pitch black. But I had matches in my pocket and I struck a light, and I found I was here, in the bivouac, and Samuel was alive and warm and sleeping next to me."

I nodded. She had finished her story. We were still sitting around the fire while Samuel slept on. Rebecca stared into the flames.

"A dream," I said.

Rebecca seemed to flinch. "No," she said. "A vision of things to come."

She believed in it then.

It's hope, I thought to myself in the silence that followed.

It's hope. The stalled plane on the ice is hope. Hope of rescue. Hope of escape.

"It keeps coming back," she said. "This story. This vision of the plane. I see it over and over again. It's like a stuck gramophone record."

Like a loop, I thought.

"I see the plane in the sky," she said, "and I lie there on the ice trying to work out how we can make it to the plane. I think maybe I can carry Samuel on my back. Or I can get to the plane myself and make them wait somehow. But I can't move, I can't get up. I'm frozen to the ice."

"It's just a dream," I said, stupidly, and Rebecca looked at me, and anger flashed briefly in her eyes.

"No," she said. "Believe me. I know that plane is coming, and I want to be on it."

"I'm sorry," I said.

She nodded. "If something happens to me," she said, "if I'm not here when the plane lands on the ice, can you do something for me?"

"What?"

"Get my little brother on that plane."

"I'll do it," I said.

"You promise?"

If she's right, I said to myself, *and the plane is real, I'll do it.*

"I promise," I said.

Twenty-nine

I went back to the antique shop in the Old Town the next day. This time I could see as I came up the cobbled street that there were lights on inside and an OPEN sign in the door.

I could see the old man, Albert, at the counter.

So he was alive. I wondered who had died.

I went in. The bell above the door clanged.

Albert recognized me. "You're back," he said.

I had the receipt with me. I put it on the counter. I came straight to the point.

"I want my coin," I said. "I came to pick it up yesterday but you were closed."

"Yes," he said. "My apologies . . . we had a death in the family."

"I'm sorry," I said. I wasn't really.

"My dog," Albert said, and he pointed behind me.

I turned and there was the little dog I'd seen here only last week. It had been alive then, but now it was dead. And somebody, perhaps Albert himself, had stuffed it. It lay curled up on a velvet pillow, eyeing me glassily over its paws, completely and utterly dead but looking for all the world as if it had just this minute sat down to have a little nap.

"Pierre," said Albert. He seemed sad.

"I am sorry," I said. And I was, a bit, this time.

"He was old," said Albert, waving away my concern. "I had been expecting it for a long time. But I took a couple of days off anyway. It means I haven't been able to value your coin just yet. Now, if you could leave it with me for another couple of days, I'm sure I could—"

"I don't want it valued," I said, interrupting him. "I just need it back. It's mine."

Albert looked at me for a moment through his glasses. I noticed that his glasses were old and a little cracked, and patched up with tape.

"Of course," Albert said and turned away from me. He began to rummage amongst the things on the workbench.

"Here it is," said Albert. He turned back toward me, holding the coin between two fingers.

My coin. Rebecca's coin. I reached for it.

"One moment," he said. He placed the coin on the glass counter between us, on its edge.

Then he set it spinning.

"This is an artifact from another time, another place," he said.

I watched the coin spin, and while I watched, Albert spoke to me. His voice was gentle, calm, and soothing. It was the voice of a hypnotist, I thought.

"Time is a river," he said, "a frozen river on which we walk. But the layer of ice that separates us from the past is paper thin."

The coin began to wobble now, spinning slower, making more noise as it did so. Albert continued, "At times you can almost see through the ice. And it can break. You can fall into the past. You can drown there, in the depths."

The coin spun to a halt and stopped.

The shop was silent, for a moment, and then I heard the clocks.

It was one o'clock. Dozens of antique clocks lined the walls, and now they chimed out the hour, on the hour, all at once. They made all kinds of different metallic sounds, some pleasant, some pure and high, and some distorted, as if the mechanism that governed them were broken or damaged.

The chimes ended and the sound of them lingered in the air, like a fading chord on an old piano.

"Did you see something on the lake?" Albert said.

I looked at him. I didn't answer. I couldn't answer.

But my lack of an answer betrayed me.

Betrayed Rebecca, perhaps.

"Did you see someone?" he asked. "Did you meet someone there, on the lake? Someone who looks like they don't belong? Someone who shouldn't be here, perhaps, at this time?"

I stared at him, my mouth open, wondering if he knew. He must have seen the surprise on my face because he moved closer, leaning forward over the counter, staring at me. I could see my own reflection, dimly, in his glasses.

"Who did you see?" he said, quite softly. "A girl? A girl, about your age?"

I recovered myself. "No," I said. "I haven't seen anybody. I haven't seen anybody out there on the lake. Anybody strange, that is."

Albert nodded. He seemed disappointed, even sad. He drew back a little.

"A long time ago," he said, "when I was a boy, I saw shadows on the lake. Spectral illuminations. Some strange combination of low winter sunlight and the ice in the air, perhaps. But they looked like people. Two children. A boy, sitting in a toboggan. And a girl pulling it."

Rebecca and Samuel, I thought.

"But they vanished," Albert continued. "They vanished whenever I took a step toward them . . . And then one day I didn't see them anymore, although I went back to look for them every year in the winter. Whenever the lake was frozen."

He smiled sadly.

"Take my advice," he said, "tread carefully on the frozen lake. It can be an unforgiving place in a winter like this. There are places where the ice is so thin a sparrow couldn't land on it without it breaking."

Thirty

That night, Rebecca was waiting for me in the woods. I came along the path I'd walked so many times in the snow, and there she was; she stepped out from behind a tree.

"Kara."

"I have something for you," I said, and I took out the coin and gave it to her. "I found it right here. In the snow."

Rebecca didn't say anything. She stared at the coin in the palm of her hand.

"What's the matter?" I said. "Is it OK? . . . I thought you'd be pleased."

A tear ran down her face.

"Maybe before I met you," she said. "Maybe before I met you I would have been pleased to get this back. But you've made me stronger than this, Kara."

Her hand closed around the coin in a fist.

"I don't need this. I don't want it. I hate it. We can survive without it."

She turned and drew her arm back, and cast the coin and all its symbols of evil into the air, and it went far and fell somewhere in the snow, somewhere over there.

It was lost, again.

It had lost.

We looked at each other, and Rebecca hugged me and kissed my cheek.

"Kara," she said. "You're my best friend."

"Am I?" I said.

"Yes," she said. "In the world. In the universe."

In the world.

In the universe.

I'd never had a friend who said things like that. It felt like fireworks inside.

We collected firewood and when our arms were full we set off for the island.

About halfway across the ice we heard a sound, out there in the darkness of the lake, and we stopped.

It was an unmistakable sound.

It was the sound of the ice breaking.

"Do you think somebody fell through the ice?" I said.

"No," said Rebecca. "Sssh . . . listen."

We listened for more breaks in the ice.

Silence.

"Maybe somebody fell through," I said.

"No," said Rebecca again. "There's nobody out here. There's only us."

I looked out into the darkness that seemed to hover over the lake and knew she was right. We were alone out here. There was no sound or sense of any other presence.

I looked at the ice beneath our feet, wondering if it was strong enough.

Rebecca put her bundle of wood down on the ice.

"I need to do something," she said. "I need to see the break in the ice. I need to see where it is."

"It's dangerous," I said.

"I know. I need it for the map."

"Be careful," I said.

"I know the ice," she said. She didn't seem afraid at all. She turned and skated away. It was as if she knew it was safe for her to go and look. It was as if she knew no harm could come to her out here, at least today, and I wondered how she knew . . .

I was struggling to make sense of these thoughts when she came back.

"Let's go," she said, picking up her wood from the ice.

"Did you see the break in the ice?" I said.

"Yes," she said, but she wouldn't look at me, and she went on, quickly, toward the island, and I had to hurry to catch up, and all the way back to the island she wouldn't look at me, and she didn't say anything either.

Something was wrong.

There was something she wasn't telling me.

Something she was afraid to tell me.

The silence between us grew longer and longer, and suddenly I felt weak and alone, and I wasn't even strong enough to ask her what was wrong.

Rebecca stopped abruptly, and I did too, and waited for her to speak.

"What would you do if I fell in the lake?" she said.

"What?"

"If the ice broke, right now, and I fell in, what would you do?"

"I'd go and get help."

"Except you can't, Kara. You can't get help. Not for me. Not for Samuel. You know that. No one must know about us."

"It's a matter of life and death," I said.

"It's always a matter of life and death," said Rebecca.

Always, I thought.

"No one else," she said. "No help. Just you."

What would you do if I fell in the lake?

I looked at the ice at my feet and thought about it.

"It's too dangerous for me to try to pull you out by myself. The ice would break beneath me too and we'd both be in trouble. We'd both drown."

"Yes," said Rebecca.

"But we have the toboggan," I said. "I could tie it to a tree on the shore and push it out to you. If you could get hold of it I might be able to pull you out."

Rebecca nodded: she was satisfied with this, pleased, even, as if I'd given her the answer to a puzzle she had been thinking about for a long time.

Thirty-one

I went to get food from the kiosk on the north shore, using my phone to light the way, looking for cracks in the ice, but it was safe: it was like skating on rock.

When I came back I found Samuel alone in the bivouac. The fire was nearly out; he'd been asleep, I think.

"Where's Rebecca?" I said.

"With you," he said, sitting up, wiping the sleep from his eyes.

The wood we'd collected was stacked nearby. Rebecca had been here but hadn't bothered to see to the fire. The toboggan was missing.

It was as if she'd gone somewhere in a hurry . . .

I handed Samuel a bag of food and he ate, and I set to tending the fire, digging out the ashes and building it up to burn through the night.

Samuel lay down again as soon as he was full, and I watched him drift off to sleep while I waited for Rebecca to come back.

There was a light sweat on his brow I saw, and he was shivering. I wondered if he was getting sick.

Perhaps the best thing to do right now was help him keep warm.

I crawled into the bivouac alongside him and snuggled up under the blanket. He was dreaming. Now and then he said single words in his sleep.

There was a name sewn into the lining of the blanket I noticed, now that I was up close with it. I ran my finger along the stitching, spelling out the word for myself in the flickering firelight.

LIEDERMAN, it said.

Then an arm came around my neck, Samuel's arm, and I slept.

I woke with sweat on my brow and I did not know how much time had passed. Samuel was beside me, sleeping, warm against my body, his head on my shoulder. I listened to the silence of the night.

The ice was creaking, far away.

Singing, Rebecca would say. *The ice was singing*.

I sat up quickly and looked around: Rebecca still had not returned.

The toboggan was still missing.

I crawled out from under Samuel without waking him.

I went to look for Rebecca.

Thirty-two

Something was wrong. I knew that as soon as I stepped out on to the ice.

The lake was different.

Or rather, the world was different.

It was darker.

I poled the ice, skating back toward the wild woods on the shore. But even the wild woods were different.

The lights of the city had vanished. No tower buildings loomed over the lake on the north shore. There was just the white of the lake under the clouds.

I stopped near the place where I usually went ashore into the wild woods, but the trees seemed wilder and darker than ever.

I was afraid now.

There were lights in the sky. Distant flashes, like sheet lightning, followed by a series of deep, percussive detonations.

I knew where I was.

I was in Rebecca's world. Rebecca's time.

I was in the war.

Real war, actual war, in the here and now.

The distant flashes and the deep sounds that came after were bombs being dropped on cities only a few miles away. And it kept happening, over and over again as more and more bombs were dropped . . .

And they fell like thunder.

It was a thousand-bomber raid.

I watched.

Then the silence came, the bombs stopped falling, and the sky in the east glowed red and orange.

The ice beneath my feet made strange creaking sounds.

Then, from out of the sky itself, came another sound.

An engine.

A British Lancaster bomber exploded out of the clouds, its four engines thrumming, on its way home. Its propellers whipped the wind, flying low.

It was a dark monster in the sky.

Ack-ack guns were firing at it still. Red tracers of flak blipped across its path, but it got through.

I saw the black mouth of the bomb-bay doors hanging open, at the ready . . .

I stared, frozen to the spot, and as the Lancaster flew directly over me, a last, stray bomb fell from the mouth of the bomb bay.

It was a dark spot coming down to earth.

Silently.

Accelerating.

It fell.

It hit the ice and punched clear through the surface.

It went on down into the water, sinking invisibly.

There was a flash of light underwater. The entire lake was lit up beneath the ice.

The power of the blast came up from the depths.

The ice cracked open, splintering into hundreds of shards fifty yards away. Water exploded up into the air. It was a fountain. A tower of water raining down, raining down on me.

I stood there in the man-made rain, trembling.

Little tides of water washed over the ice at my feet.

The ice that had supported me until now was awash.

I felt the fear of the lake coming back. The old fear-memory of almost drowning in water so cold it was painful even to hold your hand in it.

The ice beneath my feet made a strange noise.

It kind of *groaned*.

Then it kind of *creaked*.

Eeek—

Creak—

Eeek—

Creak—

I looked down. The tiny microcracks spread outward like a spider's web.

I've made a mistake, I thought, and I heard myself say the words in my head, and right then I turned and ran—or rather I skated—as fast as I could, faster than I ever had before, away from the breaking ice toward the shore, trying to put as much distance as possible between me and the hole in the lake.

Trying to outrun it.

Trying to get to firm ice . . .

I glimpsed the shore, ahead of me . . .

I skated on . . .

But the lake was faster than me.

The ice was cracking at my heels . . .

The ice was crackling . . .

The ice was crackling . . .

The next thing I knew was water.

Thirty-three

I had the strange sensation of being swallowed whole.

Swallowed alive.

The ice opened up under my feet and I went through it, and it happened so fast there was no time to think.

No time to think before the shock of the cold hit, before I gasped underwater, and when I gasped I breathed out the only air I had left in my lungs.

The last of my oxygen.

I squirmed but there was nothing to squirm against. No *down* to push down on, no *up* to pull up on. No way to tell what was up or what was down, no light, just darkness and the metallic taste of water in my mouth.

I was sinking.

There was a strange sound. For a moment I could not tell what it was or where it was coming from. Then I realized it was me.

I was screaming underwater.

A hand reached down through the hole in the ice.

I saw it—I reached for it.

It was too far away, too far up there.

I kicked my feet in the dark water and gained an inch, perhaps, and the hand reached down a little farther and that gave me another inch, perhaps, and I kicked again, darkly, below . . .

I took Rebecca's hand and she pulled me up.

Thirty-four

I was awake and I was not awake. I was cold and shivery and warm all over. There was a fire crackling somewhere nearby; I could smell the smoke, and when I opened my eyes I saw the bonfire and Samuel's and Rebecca's faces beyond it.

I was alive.

I was in the bivouac. I was wrapped up in my mother's old blue winter coat.

Rebecca had saved me from the lake. Rebecca and the toboggan, the one I'd given to Samuel. Without it, Rebecca couldn't have reached me; the ice would have broken beneath her too and we'd both have drowned. And without the toboggan's long guide rope tied fast to a tree on the shore, she'd never have been able to pull us in and we'd both have drowned, again.

But here I was. And here she was, tending the fire.

There was Samuel, examining the whistle I'd had on a string around my neck. The whistle there hadn't been any time to use when I fell through the ice. The whistle I hadn't even had time to think about before I started to drown.

My clothes were drying in the heat from the fire, propped up on sticks in a circle around it. I could see steam rising gently from my jeans.

I was down to my underwear inside the old blue winter coat, I realized. But that was what you had to do if you fell through the ice. Your clothes were soaked through, and in the cold air they'd never get dry, and nor would you, which meant hypothermia, and the body slowly shutting down due to the cold.

I was glad for the old blue coat. It was warm inside, and furry, and more like a sleeping bag than a coat, and I fell asleep again.

I drifted, warmly catching words while Rebecca and Samuel talked quietly in the light of the fire. Their voices came and went; sometimes they seemed to be far away, sometimes close by. Samuel was darning socks. Rebecca was melting water in a pot balanced at an angle over the fire.

I caught bits and pieces of a longer conversation about survival and the future, and about me.

Samuel said, "Her clothes are made in India. Did you see that?"

"Yes," said Rebecca, "and China."

They must have read the labels on my clothes.

"Everything except the blue coat," said Samuel. "That was made in Sweden."

"Yes," said Rebecca.

My mother's coat. But that was from the eighties. It was another time.

"Do you think she can help us get there?" Samuel asked.

"Where?"

"Sweden."

"Yes," said Rebecca, then, "No. I don't know."

"We have an aunt there," Samuel said.

"We do," said Rebecca, and she sighed and said, "How I've longed to be in Sweden."

They were silent then. Water came to the boil, bubbling, in the pot above the fire. I heard movement and opened my eyes to see Rebecca lift the pot off the fire and pour out two small tin cups full of steaming water for them to sip.

Sweden, I thought.

This is the place they've dreamt of.

This is where they long to be.

I've got to help them.

I startled awake in a rush that told me I'd slept for a long time, too long probably, and Samuel and Rebecca were gone.

The fire was almost out. A single small square of wood had turned into charcoal and glowed like a dark box with red edges. Smoke swirled around it strangely, pulsing and returning, as if the smoke were being drawn back into the fire, as if the wood were burning backward.

As if time were running in reverse.

I decided it was a trick of the light and my tiredness.

My clothes were there, propped up on sticks like half-scarecrows standing around the fire, and I got up and felt them.

They were dry. I climbed out of the old blue coat and quickly got dressed.

"Rebecca!" I called.

"Samuel!"

No answer. Rebecca might be fetching wood. But where was Samuel?

For a moment I thought the plane had come, the plane Rebecca said would stall and land on the ice. I thought they'd gone, already, without saying good-bye.

The thought of it made my heart sink.

Selfishly I didn't want them to have gone. I still wanted them to be here.

I saw my toboggan lying under a tree a few yards beyond the circle of fire. I took a step toward it and saw that it was half-buried in the snow.

How long had I been asleep?

How much time had passed?

Mom.

My heart sank.

Mom would have called. She'd be wondering where I was. I didn't even know what time it was. Then my hand went to my phone in my pocket and my heart sank even farther. It sank so far I felt sick, and heavy, and I wanted to cry.

My phone had been in my pocket when I went in the lake.

It had gone into the water with me.

I took it out of my pocket. The screen looked dead. I pressed the on button and waited, hoping, but nothing happened, and in my desperation I just kept pressing the on button again and again, and hoping, but nothing happened.

Mom might have called. She might be wondering where I was. I had no way of knowing.

At the lake, the world was dark. There were no tower buildings in the sky.

The sky was clear and full of stars.

I stepped out on to the ice and started walking.

I kept walking. I didn't look at the stars. I kept my head down, looking for cracks in the ice.

Every ten or twenty yards I stopped to listen to the lake. I didn't get down on my hands and knees and put my ear to the ice like Rebecca. I wouldn't know what to listen for anyway. I just listened for the telltale wash and slush of broken ice.

I listened also for the sound of the bombers in the air. I wondered if time was playing tricks on me again. If I was stuck in some kind of time loop.

If I was doomed to fall in the water again and again and again.

Then I noticed something. A glimmer of color on the ice. Like a rainbow shimmering far away, and I realized what it was: lights on the north shore.

Streetlights.

Abdul's kiosk.

Christmas lights flickered and blinked on in the trees.

Tower buildings returned to the sky.

I was back in my own time.

I reached into my pocket and took out my phone. One touch and the screen came alive, and I saw that no time at all had passed since I went out on the lake to see Rebecca this evening.

No time at all.

Mom hadn't called. She hadn't called because she hadn't missed me.

Mom didn't know.

The time I spent with Rebecca and Samuel was protected somehow, isolated, set apart from everything else.

An island in time.

Thirty-five

By day it was just an ordinary island.

I went back there as soon as it was light, hoping to find some trace of Rebecca and Samuel, some sign that they were still here, but the bivouac was empty and the fire was out, and when I took off my glove and laid my hand on the low gray hill of ashes there was no warmth there; it was as if the fire had been out for days.

"Rebecca?"

"Samuel?"

A crow cawed and took off from a tree above my head.

I saw the shape of my toboggan buried under the snow a few feet away.

The blanket was still in the bivouac though, and when I crawled inside and picked it up, there was the notebook with Rebecca's map of the ice.

So they were still here. They were still here because they needed the map. They needed the map to make their way across the ice to the plane Rebecca said was coming.

I turned the pages of the notebook, looking at the map. I was getting better at reading it now. I could see where the island was, and I could see where Rebecca had marked the ice as weak and where she thought it was strong. I could see the place where I'd fallen through the ice, which Rebecca had marked up already. I could even see the route that Rebecca planned to take, westward across the ice, to the plane.

I turned to the last page of the notebook and gasped.

There I was.

There was a drawing of me.

My face peeking out from the hood of my big winter coat.

I wasn't smiling in the drawing but I was smiling looking at it; I couldn't help myself. I sat there and stared at myself in dark pencil and I thought about Rebecca sitting here drawing me from memory by the light of the fire.

We really are friends, I thought.

I really do have a friend.

A drop of rain fell on the drawing; it landed on my penciled cheek. I looked up. Dark gray clouds had gathered in the sky; crows were circling. The weather was turning.

Belts of cold, stinging rain whipped across the lake as I set off, skating into the wind, heading home, my cheeks reddening with the pain.

I could barely see the shore. It was a hundred yards away but I kept losing it in the sleet and the snow. The air had become a perpetually falling wall of ice and hail in front of me.

I thought of Rebecca and Samuel living out here in all this terrible weather.

I couldn't do it, I thought.

I couldn't live out here.

But Rebecca had done it. Rebecca had survived.

Survival is everything, I thought.

I reached the shore.

The fight for survival.

At home, warming up with a cup of tea on my windowsill, I watched the storm turn northeast. There was a strange greenish light over the city, and the sleet slowed to nothing more than a few billowing gusts of snow, and the storm was over.

Darkness came and I looked through the telescope, looking for Rebecca.

I found her in the woods. She was collecting sticks and twigs for the fire.

I would go straight to her, I decided. But just as I was about to turn away from the telescope and get ready, I saw Rebecca do something strange.

She set her bundle of wood down in the snow and waded into a nearby snowdrift.

She lay down on her back and made a snow angel. Then she got up, dusted herself off, picked up her sticks and walked away.

What was strange about it was how I felt, watching her make this snow angel. It started as a feeling of déjà vu: I felt I'd seen this before. But I don't mean that I'd seen Rebecca making other snow angels before. What I mean is I'd seen Rebecca make *this* snow angel before. This *exact* snow angel, in this *exact* spot, and the more I thought about it, the more certain I became I'd already seen this.

It was like I was watching a repeat on TV.

It was as if Rebecca were stuck in a loop in time. An eternal loop.

Maybe that was it.

Maybe if time is a river, there can be whirlpools where time swirls around and around but never quite dissolves or disappears. And maybe there's a whirlpool around the island, and in that whirlpool there's a place where time stands still; that is, *it loops*—it repeats itself, again and again and again. A safe place, isolated from the currents of history going on all around it; a sanctuary that will last as long as the elemental forces on all sides of the whirlpool remain constant . . .

And if that were true, then Rebecca really had seen the plane that stalled in the sky. She'd seen it over and over and over again. She'd lived through it countless times. She knew what has going to happen because it already had happened.

They were stuck there, Samuel and Rebecca, alone in time.

Somehow that made me desperately sad.

I felt churned up inside.

I thought of her, out in the cold, repeating the same set of actions over and over again. I tried to imagine the loneliness. Even with Samuel to care for and to curl up with in the nights, it would have been lonelier than I could bear.

Maybe that's why Rebecca made snow angels.

Not to be alone.

I filled my backpack with things Rebecca and Samuel might need: peanut butter, cookies, cartons of juice, bread rolls. But I also packed sanitary pads for Rebecca, and some hand cream and an old pair of gloves I had. I wondered what else I could do to help.

I just wanted to make sure she'd be all right.

I zipped up my backpack and went out.

I took the stairs down to the ground floor. I wanted to get warm inside my clothes before I stepped out into the minus-degree dark.

I wasn't thinking. I didn't even look to see if the coast was clear. I just went straight out through the door of the lobby into the night.

There was someone standing across the way, smoking an electronic cigarette, alone: it was Lars.

He had his back to me but he'd heard somebody come out of the building. He turned and saw me.

I'd stopped.

"I-I-I have to go," I said.

I was stammering. I hated myself for stammering. I hated myself for being afraid.

Lars came slowly toward me.

"So go on, then," Lars said. "Go. Go past me."

I couldn't move.

I tried to move. I went right and Lars went right, into my path. I went left and Lars went left, blocking my way.

"Come on," he said. "Come on. Go past me."

I could wait, I decided.

I could go back in and wait and come out again later.

"I'm talking to you, Kara Lukas," Lars said.

That's when I turned for the door. I could hear Lars running after me, a footstep behind me, and then I heard a kind of *yelp* and he wasn't running anymore. I got to the door and punched in the code.

I was inside.

I looked back through the glass in the door.

Lars was on his knees in the snow. He'd slipped and landed on his hands and knees.

He got to his feet and looked at me.

There was no harm done. He was just angrier than ever.

I'd embarrassed him again. Like my snowball smacking him right in the face. It was the shame that made him so furious. For my part, I didn't want anything to do with him. I didn't want to talk to him or be his friend. If he simply vanished one day, I wouldn't have a problem with that. I just didn't want to have to deal with him. This animosity was all on him. It was all his choice.

My problem was that I didn't know how to extricate myself from a situation he'd created.

I watched him come slowly toward the door.

He came right up to the glass.

He looked right at me and spoke slowly.

"What's the code? What's the code for the door?"

I shook my head.

"Let me see," he said. "Is it five, six, seven, eight?"

He punched in 5678 on the keypad next to the door. Then he tried the door, rattling it.

But it remained locked.

"What's the code?"

I shook my head again.

I backed away from the glass, back toward the elevator.

I pressed the call button. I heard the elevator begin its descent, high above.

"Kara," Lars said outside, his voice muffled. He rapped on the glass of the door with his bare knuckles.

"You're going to want to see this," he said.

I looked at him and we locked eyes.

"Is it," he said, "one, three, nine, two?"

I gasped: 1392 was the code to the door.

I don't know how he'd gotten it, but he had.

I watched him now, keying in the numbers.

There was a click and Lars opened the lobby door and stepped inside.

The door *clacked* shut behind him.

He walked toward me across the space of the lobby.

I was as tall as he was. But I didn't feel as tall as him. I felt like I was shrinking as he came toward me. I felt small and I wanted to be even smaller.

I wanted to disappear, right then and there.

I felt cold all over.

I had no idea what to do. I wasn't thinking clearly. I was staring at the elevator door, praying for it to open.

Lars was standing next to me, waiting for the elevator, as if it were the most natural thing in the world.

"Please leave me alone," I said.

I could hardly breathe. My voice was kind of crushed. It was nothing more than a whisper. It didn't have any strength in it.

"What did you say?"

"I said, please leave me alone."

I saw him smile. I was looking at the blurred, fogged reflection of our faces in the metal of the elevator doors and I saw him smile, and I knew what he wanted to do to me. He didn't want to hit me or hurt me. Not necessarily. He didn't want to touch me at all, if he didn't have to. It all depended on whether or not he got what he wanted.

What he wanted was to humiliate me.

That was all. To make me feel ashamed.

To make me feel like I was lower than him.

Right then the elevator arrived.

Ping!

The doors opened.

I stepped into the elevator.

Lars stepped into the elevator alongside me.

The doors closed in front of my face.

We were inside the elevator together.

Lars didn't say anything, just waited. He was standing right behind me. I could feel him looking at me. Staring at the back of my head.

I pressed the button for the seventh floor. My floor. Then I said something stupid. I said something stupid and weak in a whispering voice.

"What floor?" I said.

Like it was a completely normal situation. Like Lars was just some other person who had gotten into the elevator at the same time as me, and because I was the nearest to the buttons on the wall, I asked him what floor he wanted. And he might have said, "Third, please," because he was on his way to see a friend who lived in my building, and if he said that, it would mean everything was normal and he wasn't going to do whatever it was he was going to do to me.

The elevator was rising.

"I'm coming with you," he said.

No hope then. My blood ran cold in my veins. The elevator was taking so long, way too long, as if time had slowed down. And I was out of ideas. I had no plan. No idea what I was going to do. No idea what was going to happen next. I had become a victim.

I'd given up.

I could hear Lars breathing behind me, a monster at my neck, standing there, close and glowering.

And then I realized something. Or rather I came to a realization that was also a kind of decision in my mind. It was an understanding I hadn't had before.

What I understood was this: the fear I felt was worse than doing something about that fear. The fear had become *so* intense, *so* crippling, that I had nothing to lose. The fear of fighting Lars was worse than *actually* fighting him.

And right then, iron entered my soul.

Viking iron.

The elevator arrived at the seventh floor.

Ping!

The doors opened and I wheeled around to face Lars with my fist already coming up toward him and I punched him. I got him right in the mouth, hard, as hard as I could, and it must have hurt him, too, because it hurt my hand.

He was surprised. Stunned, even. There was a moment when he didn't seem to understand what was happening, and that gave me time to get a second punch in, not as powerful as the first, but right on the nose, and it was then that he understood what was happening, and quickly he started pushing me back.

He was stronger than me and heavier than me and he could pretty much push me around however he liked.

Then I kind of grabbed him and pulled him close. We were scuffling, pushing and struggling, and he was stronger, but I kept elbowing him in the side and trying to kick his shins too.

The elevator doors closed.

There was a smear of blood on the mirror but I couldn't tell whether it was his blood or mine.

Ping!

The elevator door opened.

There was a voice.

"Kara!"

It was my mother.

Thirty-six

Slowly Lars and I untangled ourselves from one another. Lars looked at my mother then at the floor.

"What on earth is going on here?"

"Nothing," I said. I was looking at her. I couldn't think of anything else to say.

"Nothing? Really? You were fighting."

"Yes," I said.

"Your nose is bleeding," she said to me. "Yours, too," she said to Lars.

I put my hand to my nose. Instantly there was blood on my fingers. It was wet and dripping. I looked at myself in the mirror. There was a lot of blood on my face and neck. It was kind of smeared all down my top.

There was blood all down Lars's mouth and chin too.

I realized I'd hurt him, and I was glad.

"I was just coming to look for you," Mom said to me. "You weren't in your room, Kara."

"No," I said. "I was fighting."

"That's right," she said. "We're going to talk about this. Now go to your room."

I nodded. I stepped out of the elevator.

"What's your name?" my mother said to Lars.

"Lars Hendrikson."

"Lars Hendrikson," she said, "I know your mother."

Lars wiped his nose with his hand again. More blood came. His face was red around his left eye.

"You're going to need a tissue," she said, and she took a tissue from her pocket and handed it to him. He held it to his nose.

"Tell your mother to expect a call, Lars Hendrikson," she said.

Lars nodded.

Mom reached into the elevator and pressed the down button, and the doors closed on him.

"In your own words," Mom said.

"Yes."

"In your own time," she said.

"Yes."

"Tell me about what's happening."

I'd cleaned myself up in the bathroom. Now we were sitting at the kitchen table. The laptop—Mom's laptop—was closed. It occurred to me to say something smart and clever about how I had to get into a fight with a boy to get her to stop work and pay attention to me, but it wouldn't have been the truth. It would just have been something smart to say, and like many smart remarks, it would have taken us farther away from the truth.

That wasn't why this happened.

This wasn't Mom's fault.

This was all on Lars and I told her so.

I told her what a bully he was. The things he'd done at school. The way he'd behaved toward other boys and to girls. And I told her I wasn't going to take it anymore. I just wasn't going to allow it to go on. I had to do what I did. I had to start a fight with him.

I told her I didn't care if I got hurt. And in fact *I did* get hurt. That was my first fight ever—and it was a draw—and I'm OK with that because winning wasn't the point. I was never going to win this fight because he's stronger than me and heavier than me.

The point was to show him I'm not afraid of him. The point was to show him if he tries to bully me again, I'm going to hit him. Hard. The point was to show him he can't humiliate me or make me feel like I'm lower than him.

Because I'm not lower than him.

I'm not lower than anybody.

I'm as good as anybody in the world.

Mom looked at me for a long time after I'd said that. She was kind of staring at me. I didn't have any idea how she was going to react.

"Kara," she said, "you are a very brave young woman. I am so proud of you and what you've done tonight. I give you my blessing and my permission, not that you need it, to go on being you. I don't want you to fight. But I understand. *I know*, there are times when you have to fight. When *not to* fight is the wrong thing to do. And I trust your instincts. I'm grateful that you're you, Kara, and I love you."

She was in tears. I was too.

We hugged.

That night I slept and dreamt of Rebecca.

Thirty-seven

I let myself into the old house. No one had answered when I'd knocked. That wasn't unusual, though.

"Grandpa?"

I put my bag down in the hall. Then I went along the passageway.

"Grandpa?"

"In here," came his voice.

I went into the kitchen. He was there, pouring himself a cup of coffee from the pot. He brought out a soft drink for me and a large piece of cake for us to share.

We sat down at the table. For a while neither of us said anything.

I knew he knew about the fight. My mother had called him, late last night, and told him about it. I knew he'd have been as proud of me as she was. He might not be able to say it, but he'd be proud that I'd fought like a Viking. Proud that I'd made myself feared.

There he was, sitting across the table from me, smiling in his own shy way.

But there were other things we needed to talk about.

For one thing, I needed to tell someone what was happening to me. I needed to tell someone about the strange, magical things I was experiencing. Not the whole story, of course: I wasn't going to tell anyone about Rebecca and Samuel and the island. But I needed some answers and Grandpa was the person to tell, if I was going to tell anyone.

The only trouble was I didn't know how to begin.

I looked at the table, at the grain of the old wood there.

I looked at the knot in the wood and thought of the whirlpool in time.

I said, "Do you think you can meet someone from another time?"

He nodded then, as if he'd been expecting the question for a long time—maybe not today but sometime. Then he said, "Hmm," and nodded again.

He poured more coffee carefully into his cup.

"I believe in light," he said. "I believe in the stars . . . how late we see the light they emanate. How much time has passed since they shone. Perhaps that's what time travelers are, Kara. Perhaps that's what ghosts are, too. Just light arriving a little too late. Light falling through time to illuminate the present. Light that needs to be seen. So it can go on its way through the universe."

Yes, I thought to myself.

Yes.

That's exactly what Rebecca is.

Light that needs to be seen.

Perhaps that's why I'd only ever seen her at night. The days were too bright, her light too faint. She could only shine against a background of darkness.

My cell phone rang, faintly, muffled.

It was in my bag in the hall.

I recognized the ringtone I'd set for my mother.

"Just a minute," I said to Grandpa.

I went out into the passageway and rummaged around in my bag until I found the phone and answered it.

"Hey, Mom," I said into the phone.

"Where are you?" she said.

"I'm at Grandpa's house," I said. I was looking at myself in the old mirror in the hallway.

"OK," she said, and then, "Um. Uh. You need to come to the hospital now."

"The hospital?" I said.

"Yes," she said. "I'm going to call a taxi. It's going to come right to where you are and pick you up."

I was worried now.

"But why do I need to come to the hospital?"

"Just—just call me when you're in the taxi, OK?"

"Tell me," I said.

"Kara," she said. Her voice was serious. It was a tone of voice I hadn't heard from her in a long time. "I need you to do what I say. Call me when you're in the taxi."

"All right," I said.

She ended the call.

I went back along the passageway.

When I came into the kitchen, Grandpa wasn't there.

He was gone, and it didn't look like he had been here at all.

Not recently.

Not today, at any rate.

The coffee pot stood where it always stood on the sideboard. It was clean and empty and cold when I put my hand on it.

Grandpa's cup—the cup I'd just seen him bring to his lips so he could blow on his coffee—was hanging in its spot from the shelf above the counter.

I took it down and felt it in my hands.

It was cold.

I looked at the table. There was my glass of juice. There was the plate and the crumbly remains of the cake we'd shared, and a single fork.

The chair Grandpa had been sitting in was pulled up close to the table.

I knew why we had to go to the hospital today. I knew what had happened. I knew what I'd learn at the hospital.

I went to the kitchen window and looked out at the back garden under the snow, and at the old wooden jetty, and at the frozen lake beyond.

A car horn beeped.

The taxi had arrived.

Thirty-eight

Grandpa had died. He was in a hospital bed with a sheet pulled up to his neck.

He'd fallen in the early hours of the morning, a nurse said, at home, on the stairs. He'd managed to telephone for an ambulance himself. Then he'd lapsed into unconsciousness before they'd been able to contact Mom. Or me.

The nurse who told us this had been with him when he died. She'd held his hand. His chest had risen and fallen, risen and fallen, and then was still.

It was likely a bleed in the brain caused by the fall. He wouldn't have known anything about it.

Mom arrived a little later.

I came shortly after that.

He was dead before I arrived at the old house and spoke with him there. Before we spoke about ghosts. Before he told me about light that needs to be seen so it can go on its way through the universe.

I held his hand. I whispered in his ear, "Thank you."

I said, "Go on your way through the universe."

Mom overheard me.

"What did you say to him?" she said.

I told her.

"Yes," she said. "Yes. That's it."

She looked at her father lying there. "You can go on your way through the universe now," she said.

I squeezed her hand.

Now we were two.

Just me and her.

Thirty-nine

Mom cooked. We ate our pasta and herbs in tomato sauce in silence.

She set the dishwasher running quietly.

I sat at the table with my hands cupped around a hot chocolate.

Doing nothing, thinking nothing, feeling everything.

Like every cell of my body was electrified with loss.

Lit up with the knowledge he was gone.

Then something happened that called me back to the here and now.

The telephone rang.

The landline. And Mom and I both had the same thought.

Only one person ever calls us on the landline.

Grandpa.

I got up, and walked over, and picked up the receiver.

"Hello?"

It was Lars's mother. She wanted to talk to Mom.

I put my coat on and went out.

Forty

I decided I would make a snow angel.

That's what I told Mom I was going to do anyway. I had my backpack with me, full of supplies for Rebecca and Samuel. I went down to the wild woods. It was late in the afternoon and already dark, and I was alone.

It was just me and the moonlight and the crows.

I came to a big rising bank of fresh snow and that's where I lay down and made the snow angel.

I remained there on my back and looked at the sky. There were a few stars and a waxing moon. I had some idea Grandpa was up there now, a piece of pure light traveling through the universe. If he looked back at this planet, I wanted him to see the angel I'd made looking back up at him.

He was gone forever.

I was never going to see him again.

There was the sound of boot crunch on snow, and I turned my cheek to the cold and looked.

Rebecca emerged from behind a stand of trees. She looked guilty, as if she'd been watching me for some time.

I didn't get up.

"You know what?" I said. "I wish you'd tell me how you do it."

"Do what?" said Rebecca.

"Make the snow angels."

"Make snow angels?" said Rebecca. "I don't understand. You lie down in the snow . . ."

"I mean without leaving any footprints."

Rebecca frowned.

"No footprints?" she said. "That would be impossible, wouldn't it?"

I sat up. "Rebecca," I said. "Please. Tell me how you do it."

"I've made snow angels but it's not magic, Kara," said Rebecca. "You just lie down in the snow, and . . . you know."

She didn't know what I was talking about.

Now I didn't know what to think.

"Unless it's not you," I said. "Unless it's someone else . . . I give up."

I lay back flat in the snow, looking up at the trees and the stars. I heard movement and then Rebecca appeared, standing above me, looking down at me. And then, very gently, she said,

"Has something happened, Kara?"

"My grandpa died," I said.

"I'm sorry," said Rebecca.

"You don't need to be," I said, and I meant it. She'd lost everybody—everything. She'd lost the past, her parents, grandparents, everyone she'd ever known, and she'd lost the future, the life to come. There was only the now.

There was only the task: keep Samuel alive.

"Help me up," I said. I reached out a hand, expecting Rebecca to take it and pull me to my feet, but she didn't, and when I looked where she'd been standing a moment ago, there was nobody there.

"Rebecca?" I said. I sat up.

There was no sign of her.

I got to my feet and brushed the snow off my clothes.

"Rebecca?"

I heard a muted *CRACK!* far away.

A gunshot.

Somewhere out there on the lake.

I started to walk down to the shore.

I was still not quite sure what I'd heard.

My pace quickened.

If it really was what it sounded like.

I had an awful feeling.

A really awful feeling.

I was running.

I ran.

*

I skated toward the island. There were hundreds of crows in the trees there, outlined darkly, and as I came closer they took off en masse and filled the sky above me, cawing.

"Rebecca!" I called.

"Rebecca!"

I couldn't see her anywhere. Then, faintly, I heard a high shrill sound.

A whistle.

Someone blowing on the little toy whistle.

Rebecca.

I followed the sound, nearer and nearer.

"Rebecca?" I said.

The whistle stopped, and a hundred yards from the island, there was an answer.

"Kara . . ."

It was Rebecca. Her voice was weak. It sounded like she was in pain.

Then I saw her: a dark shape on the ice.

I skated toward her. She was lying down on the ice. Lying motionless.

I came to her. Her eyes were closed.

"Rebecca!" I shouted.

Her eyes opened and she looked at me.

"Kara," she said. "I fell . . ."

I put my arms around her and tried to get her to sit up, but I couldn't. She had no strength. It was like she had nothing left. Her bare hand opened and the toy whistle slipped out on to the ice. But there was no blood that I could see. No sign of injury. I didn't understand what was happening.

"Kara," she said, "you came."

"I heard you," I said.

"You came," she said. "It's different . . . It's different this time."

"Rebecca," I said. "Rebecca, what happened?"

Her eyes closed and I brushed her hair away from her face, and then she opened her eyes again, but this time she wasn't looking at me.

"Look, Kara," she said. "The stars!"

I looked up.

The glow of the city was gone, again. It was as if another dark power cut had swept across the land.

The stars were out.

We were in Rebecca's time, not mine.

Meteors fell in the sky. The Quadrantids.

"I dreamt I came down from the stars," said Rebecca. "I walked in the snow on the rooftops of a strange city. I was weightless. I made angels in the snow. I made a friend, a girl. Her name was Kara."

"I'm your friend," I said. "I'm your friend forever."

Rebecca smiled and looked at me then. "I heard you singing, Kara. I heard you singing when you walked in the woods by the shore. I listened to your song."

I held her in my arms.

"I wish you long life, Kara," she said. "I wish you long life."

Something warm and wet trickled through the gap between my glove and my sleeve, and right then I knew what had happened.

I didn't need to look.

I'd heard something that sounded like a gunshot.

That's exactly what it was.

Rebecca hadn't slipped: she'd been shot.

She's dying, I thought, and I took off my glove and reached for her hand, and held her bare hand in my bare hand.

"It's different this time," she said.

"I'm here," I said.

"No," she said. "Listen . . . there's nothing in the sky."

For a moment I didn't understand what she meant, and then I remembered the plane. The plane she'd said would come: the plane that would stall in the sky. And I understood how she'd known about the plane: she'd seen it all before. She'd lived through this. Time turned back on itself like a figure eight, and went around again.

Except this time the sky was silent. There was no plane.

"I was wrong," she said, "it's all been for nothing."

"It can't be," I said. But I looked at the sky and she was right. There were only stars.

She seemed to see something then, far away, across the ice.

"Look," she said. "Look."

I couldn't see anything where she was looking.

"What is it?" I said. "What do you see?"

"It's a candle," she said, and smiled. That was the last thing she said.

Something happened in her eyes. They darkened and clouded while I watched.

"Rebecca," I said.

"Rebecca," I said again.

"Talk to me."

"Please, Rebecca."

"Look at me."

She didn't close her eyes. But she didn't look at me either.

"Please, Rebecca," I said. "Please . . . Live . . . Please live. You can't go. You can't . . ."

But she was gone.

Anger surged inside me.

"But I don't have any friends!" I shouted, to the night, to the world, to the universe. I looked up at the stars and shouted right up at them. "I don't have any friends! Don't you understand? I don't have any friends! I don't have anyone in the world!"

The stars looked down on me, cold and unfriendly, and didn't answer.

I was crying, I noticed. I had been crying for some time.

I closed Rebecca's eyes.

I stayed with Rebecca for a long time, holding her in my arms, cradling her.

It was cold but I no longer cared.

I couldn't bring myself to move.

Far above me in the sky I heard a sound.

A distant thrumming hum.

An engine.

A plane, somewhere up there.

But it was more than that.

It was hope.

I looked up and I saw it.

It was as Rebecca said it would be.

It was a smaller and lighter and faster plane than the Lancaster bomber I'd seen.

It was flying low.

Its twin engines coughed—once, twice—and one spluttered and stalled.

Exactly as Rebecca had foretold.

The plane went on, gliding free in the air.

Looking for somewhere to land.

And I knew.

I knew what I had to do.

I laid Rebecca down gently on the ice.

I saw the toy whistle and picked it up.

I would never have found her without it. I would never have seen her again.

I ran quickly back to the island, through the trees, to the bivouac.

Samuel was there. He was wide-eyed and awake, sitting by the fire. He was waiting for me. He'd heard the plane too. He was holding the map of the ice in his hands.

Forty-one

I carried Samuel back to the shore. He was heavy. Heavier than I thought a kid could be. We stumbled once or twice on the ice. We slipped in the snow. But we kept going.

We came to where I'd left the toboggan. I set him down on the ground and then I untied the toboggan and brought it to him. He had my backpack on his back. It contained some things he might need, and the map.

He had the old checked blanket in his hands. It was like he was clinging to it. I took it from him gently and laid it over his knees and tucked him in.

"You have to keep warm," I said.

"Yes," he said. His teeth were chattering.

I hugged him.

"Where's Rebecca?" he said.

I drew back. When I spoke, the lie came out as smoothly as the truth.

"She's waiting for us at the plane," I said. I looked into Samuel's eyes. "She went ahead of us to make sure they don't leave without you."

Samuel looked at me with watchful, unblinking eyes, and then he said, quite calmly, "OK. Let's go."

I was not sure he believed me. I wondered how much he really knew, or even wanted to know.

I got to my feet.

I gripped the guide rope in my hands and put my back into it and pulled, and the toboggan moved.

Then I stopped.

I stopped because something else had happened.

There was a gunshot, or something that sounded like a gunshot, and when I turned and looked back, east across the lake, I saw a firework in the sky.

Not a firework. I knew that now.

"A flare," said Samuel.

"Yes," I said.

"We have to go," Samuel said.

"I know," I said. But I couldn't move. Not yet. I needed to see where the flare fell so I could get as far away from it as possible, so that whoever was out there on the lake, whoever was hunting us, wouldn't be able to see us.

The flare had turned in the sky and was falling now, yellow, illuminating the ice for about half a mile all around. Down it came, finally, spitting yellow flames, landing way too close to us: a mere two hundred yards away.

"Kara," said Samuel.

"Yes," I said, but I couldn't move. I was looking back across the ice to where Rebecca's body lay, visible now at the border of the flare's lurid light.

She lay still, just a dark smudge on the ice.

Samuel didn't look back.

Something told me he knew what was there, behind him.

"Kara," he said again.

"Yes," I said, and I turned and began to pull, and said, "Let's go."

The flare had fallen on the east side of the island. So we went west, quickly. I took us around the island and into the shadow of the western side, where the island itself hid us from the flare.

I pulled on, into the darkness. The toboggan went quickly over the ice. I began to think, *We're making good time.* I began to think, *We can make it.* Then I heard the sound of an engine, distantly at first, moving along the north shore, steadily coming closer. There were no lights that I could see: I assumed they'd switched their headlights off to hide their position. Then the engine sound changed, and slowed, and the vehicle came to a halt.

I stopped and beside me the toboggan stopped, and we both watched the tree line on the north shore.

There was a faint electrical humming sound and a bright circle of light appeared in the trees: a searchlight about a mile away, mounted on the back of a vehicle on the shore.

The light blazed and swept across the lake, scanning the ice, sweeping past the island. I held my breath. We were totally exposed out here on the ice. There was no shelter; there was no hiding place.

The great white beam of light reached us, and passed over us, and I thought for a moment that they hadn't seen us, that we'd been too small and far away, too insignificant for them to bother with. But the searchlight stopped and came back across the ice, and found us again.

One moment we had been in the dark, the next we were outlined in bright white light. It was fantastically bright. I shaded my eyes with my hand, to try to see what they were going to do now. I tried to listen, too: to listen for dogs.

Samuel said, "Someone's coming."

I didn't reply; I was staring into the searchlight.

"Someone's coming," said Samuel, again.

"Where?" I said. "I don't see anyone."

"Not there," said Samuel. "Behind us."

I heard skates then, and I turned and looked back, and there was someone coming.

A boy.

A boy alone on the ice, skating toward us.

I knew who it was.

It was Lars.

"Who is it?" said Samuel.

"Not a friend," I said.

Samuel nodded, watching Lars, approaching. "What does he want?"

"I don't know," I said.

I really didn't know.

I was too tired to fight him, if that's what he wanted.

But I would, if I had to. Again.

Lars skated closer, then slowed and stopped about ten yards away. He looked at me, then looked at the toboggan, then back at me. He was standing right in the beam of the searchlight, but I don't think he even saw it.

I don't think he saw Samuel either.

"What are you doing out here?" he said.

I shook my head.

Not telling.

"What are *you* doing out here?" I said.

"I saw you in the woods," he said.

"You followed me."

"Yes," he said. "I saw you make a snow angel."

"You were spying on me."

"No," he said, and then, "Yes. Sorry. I just wanted to say . . ." He trailed off.

I waited. I thought about the plane that had landed on the ice. I wondered how long they'd be there, stuck on the ice. I wondered how long it'd take to fix an engine. A few hours, maybe. And they weren't going to wait.

Nothing about this was going according to plan.

"What I mean is . . . What I mean to say is, I—uh . . ." Lars stumbled over his words.

"We don't have time for this," said Samuel, as if he and I were thinking the same thought.

"No," I said.

"We have to go," said Samuel.

"Yes," I said.

Lars looked at me like I was crazy, like I was talking to myself.

"Go home," I said to him. "This has nothing to do with you."

I put my weight into the guide rope and went forward, and pulled. The toboggan moved. Slowly at first, but it began to pick up speed, carried along by my momentum. I took us farther out onto the lake, away from the island, out toward the middle of the ice. The searchlight beam moved with us, tracking us, and Lars followed us too, skating along beside me, bewildered.

Samuel turned to face backward in the toboggan, his eyes on the north shore, watching, listening. There was another sound then, coming across the lake from somewhere behind the glare of the searchlight, and I knew what it was, and I knew what it meant.

Dogs.

Dogs, barking, yelping, waiting to be released.

Dogs.

"Do you hear that?" said Samuel.

"I hear it," I said.

"Hear what?" said Lars, skating alongside.

"They're going to set the dogs on the ice," said Samuel.

"Yes," I said. I didn't look back; I just kept going on.

"They're going to hunt us down," said Samuel.

"Yes," I said.

"Then what happens?" said Samuel.

I didn't answer. I had no answer. This was not the way it was supposed to go.

"Kara," said Samuel.

I didn't answer.

"Kara," said Samuel. "We have to stop."

What?

I wasn't going to stop. That was the only thought in my head.

Don't stop and don't look back.

Keep going.

If you don't stop, the distance between you and the plane keeps shrinking.

If you don't stop, at least you have a chance.

"Stop," said Samuel, and then, "Kara, please. Stop."

I stopped.

I looked back at Samuel on the toboggan. I wondered if this was the end. If part of him, somewhere inside him, had given up all hope.

"What's going on?" said Lars. He had stopped too and was close to me now, and I didn't like him being there.

Samuel pointed to Lars and said, "Show him."

Show Lars.

Show Lars the searchlight that shines on his face.

Show him, so he can hear the dogs out there.

The dogs they're going to set on our trail.

"Show him," said Samuel. "It's our only chance."

I could see he was right.

No matter how much I hated Lars, we needed him.

I turned to face Lars and said quickly, "Are you sorry about what you did?"

Lars's mouth opened in surprise, but he swallowed and nodded and said, quietly, "Yes."

I nodded. I took off my glove and held out my hand.

"Call it quits then," I said. "We're even. Shake."

Lars looked at my bare hand waiting there in the cold and understood. He took his glove off his right hand and reached out and shook my hand.

We touched.

He gasped.

He felt the glare of the searchlight on his face, and turned to look at it, over there in the trees. He heard the barking of the dogs in the faraway dark. He saw Samuel sitting in the toboggan, the toboggan he'd thought was empty.

He saw that the searchlight had us pinned to the ice.

"What's going on?" he said.

"There's no time to explain," I said. "We need your help."

Forty-two

Lars took out his penknife and opened the blade.

He took the guide rope from me and cut it in two.

His hands were shaking, I saw. He was scared. I'd told him what was happening. Where we were and *when* we were, and what we had to do.

He picked up the severed half of the guide rope and retied it to the toboggan; Samuel watched him do it and when he was done, their eyes met for a moment.

"Hello," said Lars.

Samuel nodded hello back.

Now we had two guide ropes. We could both pull the toboggan at the same time. We could go faster. It was a chance.

"Let's go," said Lars.

I saw Samuel smile, and that was the last thing I saw for a while.

There was a *CLUNK!* and the searchlight was turned off and we were blinded by the dark.

"What does that mean?" said Lars.

It means they're going to release the dogs, I thought, but I didn't say it.

"It means we have to go," I said and I took the strain of the guide rope, and Lars did the same, and the toboggan moved.

We put our backs into it.

The toboggan slid across the ice, faster this time.

Not fast enough, I thought. *We'll never outrun the dogs.*

The toboggan ran swiftly across the ice.

For a moment it was quiet on the lake. Almost peaceful. There was just the sound of our skates on the white surface. Just the sound of the toboggan. Then behind us there was the sound of the dogs being set loose on the lake, barking and howling, spreading out across the ice.

"They're coming," said Samuel, and Lars slowed and stumbled, and looked back, but I took his arm and steadied him, and we went on.

Samuel kept watch. The sound of the dogs came in waves, over the ice.

Still, they were too far away to see.

Slowly, in the darkness and vastness of the frozen lake, but surely, the dogs were gaining on us. They were faster than us, even if the ice was not their best terrain, even if they slipped and skidded almost as much as we did.

They were relentless.

"They're coming," Samuel said again.

"Yes," I said. I didn't know what to do.

"We have to get off the ice," said Lars. "We have to get to the shore and hide."

"We can't hide from them," I said.

"I can see them," said Samuel. "I can see them now."

He was facing backward in the toboggan and there—behind him—on the moonlit ice, were the shapes of the dogs, running us down.

We could hear them coming, louder and louder, moving inexorably closer with every passing second, racing toward us across the ice.

"What do we do?" said Samuel.

"I don't know," I said.

"We can't outrun them," said Lars.

"I know that," I said, and right then I stopped, and Lars stopped, and the toboggan carrying Samuel slowed to a halt on the ice.

I looked back at the dogs.

"We can split up," said Lars. "You go that way. I'll go this way. I'll take the toboggan."

"Wait," I said. "Let me think."

It's over, I thought. My mind raced. *It's over.*

Wait. The map.

"The map," I said.

"What?" said Lars.

"The map," I said, and Samuel understood, and quickly opened the backpack and took out the notebook. I went to him and we opened the map, and I scanned it and found what I was looking for.

"Here," I said to Lars. "Look."

"What is it?"

"It's a map of the ice," I said. "It shows where it's strong and where it's weak. The dogs are there. And I think we're here." I tapped my finger on the map.

"So we go that way," said Lars, pointing north.

"Yes," I said. I threw the map to Samuel, who caught it, and Lars and I grabbed the guide ropes and pulled.

Pulled hard.

Pulled for our lives.

We set off at an oblique angle to our original course. The dogs, behind us, followed suit, turning north to intercept us. Then I took us by a zigzag route across the ice. There was one particular patch of scribblings Rebecca had made on the map that I wanted to lead them to.

The dogs followed. If we turned this way, they turned this way. If we turned that way, they turned that way. They had our scent. We were the only living things out here on the ice. They knew exactly where we were as surely as if the searchlight were shining on us.

"Keep going," I said to Lars.

"I am keeping going," he said.

"Trust me," I said.

"I do," he said.

The dogs came ever closer. We could hear the skittering of their claws on the ice now.

Then we were where I wanted us to be.

"Here," I said. "Stop. Wait."

The toboggan slid to a stop beside us.

Samuel looked down at the ice and listened.

The ice was creaking.

Tiny microcracks appeared in the surface.

Forty-three

Far away another flare appeared in the sky, rising green like a firework above the lake, and we could see the dogs now, a dozen of them, fifty yards away, half-starved but strong and snarling, coming at us, terrifyingly loud and deadly.

But the ice beneath them was deadlier.

We heard the *CRACK* as the ice gave way.

One moment our ears were ringing with their barks, the next there was only a confused, muted yelping. The dogs slowed and slipped and skidded, as crack after crack opened in the black and watery surface beneath them.

A hole in the ice, dark, like a mouth, opened under the three dogs at the front of the pack and swallowed them. They went down and under, and bobbed up and swam around looking for a way out of the water. Behind them, the remains of the pack had stopped. They were confused and afraid. They trod warily across the ice, trying to retrace their steps. Here and there the ice broke again and a forepaw sank down, and a dog yelped and scrambled away, shivering, chastened.

The flare fell toward us. We could see everything now: the blackness of the water, the ice beneath our feet.

It did not look that safe to us.

"We have to go," I said to Lars.

"Yes."

"The ice!" I said.

"Yes!" he said.

Right then the flare landed, as if it had been perfectly aimed, slap bang between us and the dogs, and it went into the water, and carried on burning as it went down, illuminating the world beneath the surface of the lake, burning in the depths, going down and down through the silt and the murky sludge until it disappeared finally, extinguished, sixty yards down.

There was a silence then, and when we looked back across the ice we saw that the dogs were out of the water now, all of them, I think, and they were standing just across the gap in the ice from us, staring, silent.

A narrow channel of dark water had spread across the lake. The dogs were marooned on their side. There was no way they could follow us.

We turned and went on, pulling the toboggan. And behind us the dogs howled and howled and howled.

Forty-four

We went on without a word.

There was just the *pock-pock-pock* of our poles on the ice. Just the sound of the toboggan behind us. Just the push of our breath in the air.

Samuel was sitting up in the toboggan, his hands clutching the sides for stability. His bright-dark eyes were open, watching us, watching the stars.

I hadn't told him yet about Rebecca.

I hoped somehow I wouldn't have to.

Lars was next to me, pulling as hard as I was.

We were silent.

I was silent.

I didn't tell him I'd had my fingers crossed behind my back when we shook hands. I didn't tell him I hadn't forgiven him.

This is only a truce, I told myself.

Above us a crow flew silently by. I looked up and saw that the moon was full now, bright, beaming down upon us like a lamp.

I saw something ahead on the ice.

A great dark shape.

We came closer, and slowed, and finally we stopped.

It was the plane.

The great dark shape was an airplane parked on the ice. It was the plane I'd seen flying low overhead, the plane that had stalled in the air.

It stood there in silence. There were no lights on anywhere that we could see. We wondered if there were any crew aboard.

Lars and I walked beneath the wings. It was a dark and giant beast, towering over us, blocking out the sky with its wings. I placed my hand on the fuselage and felt the cold black metal.

By contrast the ice was luminous in the moonlight.

"Where are we?" Lars whispered. "What is this?"

I put a finger to my lips.

Trust me.

Samuel waited in the toboggan. I saw a crow land on the ice near him, and he looked at the crow and nodded to it, and the crow took off again.

I walked over to Samuel. He smiled at me.

"You have to go now, Kara," he said. "You shouldn't be here. Either of you. You must go."

Lars came out from under the wing.

A breeze rustled the trees on the shore a mile away.

I went to Samuel and hugged him.

"Good-bye," I said.

"Good-bye, Kara," he said.

I didn't talk to him about Rebecca then. I didn't tell him what had happened to her. But I think he knew. I think somehow he had always known.

I looked into Samuel's eyes.

"I wish you long life," I said. It was what Rebecca had said to me, just hours ago.

"Thank you," said Samuel.

He looked at Lars and nodded. It was just a little nod of the head, to show respect, and Lars nodded back to him, and our good-byes were over.

There was a *clang* as a door swung open in the side of the plane. Yellowy light spilled out on to the ice, and a British RAF pilot in full flying gear stepped out. He went quickly to the front of the plane and removed the wooden chocks from beneath the wheels.

The ice creaked beneath his feet.

He heard a whistle: a quiet, high, short sound, and he froze, and turned slowly, as if he were expecting to see guns pointing at his back. Instead he saw nothing.

Then he heard a child's voice, a voice that was weak with fatigue.

"Help," said the child. "Help me . . . Help."

The pilot walked back around the plane, looking for the child whose voice he'd heard. He stepped out from under the wing and saw a smallish bundle of something out there on the ice. He did not know what he was looking at.

Samuel blew the whistle once more, and the pilot came closer and saw the boy in a blue coat, wrapped in an old checked blanket, sitting on the ice.

"Who are you?" the pilot said.

"I'm a refugee," said Samuel.

"Are you indeed?"

"Yes," Samuel said. "I've been hiding. Here. On an island on the lake. For two years. I can't stay here."

"Why not?" said the pilot.

"I'm a Jew," said Samuel.

The pilot seemed to think about this for a moment.

"Very well," he said. "You'd better come with us. I think we've room for one more."

"There's something else," said Samuel, quickly.

"What?" said the pilot.

"I can't walk," said Samuel.

"How the devil did you get here?" asked the pilot.

"I had help," said Samuel. He smiled. "I had friends. They brought me here."

We had heard every word in the uncanny silence of the lake.

We stood some distance away.

But we could see tears shining in Samuel's eyes.

The pilot went to him and said something else, close by, something I didn't catch, and then in one smooth movement the pilot picked Samuel up, hoisting him up into the safety of his arms.

He carried Samuel back to the plane and steered him gently through the open door.

The plane's engines started. They were louder, I think, than anything I'd ever heard before; we were still so close to it. The propellers whirred. We caught one last glimpse of Samuel, inside the plane, and then the pilot climbed in after him, and pulled the door shut.

Darkness and moonlight and the sound of the engines . . .

The plane began to move.

It turned a hundred and eighty degrees on the ice, and taxied, rattling and bouncing up and down on the ice, engines roaring . . .

Finally it was airborne, and away to safety.

Forty-five

"We're lost, aren't we?"

"No," I said. *I lied.*

We were lost.

I'd been preparing for this. I had all sorts of explanations ready, all sorts of excuses, but Lars simply took my word for it that we weren't lost, and on we went.

The woods where we walked were wild and dark. There were no streetlights. No skyglow of a distant city. No faint hum of faraway traffic.

Snow covered the paths beneath our feet, if indeed there were paths there. We trudged on through the snow dragging the toboggan behind us.

I hoped we were back in our own time, although how much time had passed, if any, I didn't know.

I didn't even know what year it was.

Lars walked in silence beside me. He was burning with questions he was too tired to ask and I was too tired to answer.

I hadn't forgotten what he had done. I hadn't forgotten what I owed him, but equally I hadn't forgotten what he'd done to me.

I found it hard to reconcile the Lars walking beside me in the snow with the Lars of just a few days ago.

Maybe he did too. Maybe he was struggling to find the words.

So we went on in silence, growing more and more tired with every step, getting colder with every passing minute.

"We're lost, aren't we?" said Lars a little later.

"No," I said, lying.

We could be anywhere. We could be lost in time. We could meet Vikings. We might never get home.

All I knew was that it was night and that we could not go on forever in this cold.

Lars had stopped; this time he was not convinced.

"Where are we, then?" he said.

"The wild woods," I said. "I know these trees."

"Which way is home?"

"The way we're going," I said, pointing vaguely ahead of us.

"How far is it, then?"

"Two or three miles," I said. "It's going to take us an hour."

"You're sure?"

"I promise," I said, fingers crossed.

I didn't want him to know we were lost. I didn't want him getting any crazy ideas. I didn't want him to panic. I didn't want him going off on his own.

Our best chance of getting home safely was sticking together.

I was thinking about what I was going to say to him when he realized I was lying about being lost, when something else happened and he panicked anyway.

We were not alone in the woods.

There was somebody walking ahead of us.

Walking toward us actually.

I stopped, assuming Lars was right beside me, and then I saw who it was on the path ahead of us, and I gasped.

It was Lars.

I turned my head and looked where Lars had been walking up until a moment ago, and he was gone. There were his tracks in the snow and there they ended, and here I was, alone.

I looked at the other Lars a hundred yards away in the snow.

He'd stopped and seemed to be peering out into the darkness.

He looked scared and confused.

I heard him shout.

"Kara!"

"I'm coming."

I walked toward him through the snow.

"Kara!"

“I’m right here,” I said. “I’m coming.”

“KARA!”

I stopped. It was as if he hadn’t heard me. And he was spooked. I could see it in his face. I could hear it in his voice.

“Who’s there?” he said. “Is there somebody there? Kara, where are you?”

He was looking right through me. I was standing at the edge of the circle of light thrown by the streetlight above him. We were only a few feet apart. He should have been able to see me. And yet it was as if I weren’t there.

“I’m here,” I said. “Lars. Can you see me? Can you hear me?”

He didn’t say anything.

“Hey,” I said. “Lars. Snap out of it. Come on.”

He didn’t say anything, again.

He didn’t see me. He didn’t hear me.

Somehow we’d slipped out of sync in time.

Where are we now?

I took a step toward him, into the circle of light, and Lars took a sudden, startled step back. He was staring at the ground beneath my feet. At my footprints, which to his eyes had simply appeared, magically, in the snow.

I took another step forward, and Lars took another step back.

“Please don’t do that,” he said. “Whoever you are.”

I stopped.

“Is it you, Kara?” He was looking right through me.

“It’s me,” I said, though I knew he couldn’t hear me.

"Kara?"

Take his hand, I thought. *Take his hand, and he'll be able to see you.*

Except we're both wearing gloves. And this needs touch.

Lars groaned.

"Lars," I said, "I'm right here. Don't be afraid."

"Who's there?" said Lars.

"It's me," I said.

"Who's there?" he said again. "Is there somebody there? Kara?"

"I'm right here," I said. I realized I wanted him to know I was there, somehow. Like Rebecca. To be aware of my presence. My soul.

But perhaps that was just me and Rebecca.

"I'm here," I said, and I took a step toward him and he saw my footprints appear in the snow, and he screamed and stumbled backward, and fell and landed on his backside. But I just kept coming, just kept walking through the snow toward him, and he scrabbled and kicked and slipped and just couldn't get to his feet.

"Stop it!" he said. "Please. Whoever you are, just STOP IT!"

I stopped right in front of him.

He was shaking, quaking, his eyes darting here to there. All I had to do was take his hand.

Instead I waited.

I found I had some small, thin thread of cruelty in my soul. Some desire for revenge?

Lars had helped me. Saved me. But before that, we'd had a fight. And I was not quite ready to call it quits, even now. I wanted more. I wanted to see what he was made of. I wanted to know what he was going to do now.

"Kara, please," he said. "Please, wherever you are. Kara, please. I'm scared, Kara. I'm scared."

I didn't answer.

"Kara," he said. "I'm sorry. I'm sorry. I'm sorry I bullied you. I'm so sorry . . ."

He trailed off. Tears ran quietly down his cheeks.

"You're stronger than me, Kara," he said, quietly. "You're stronger than me."

All right. Quits. For real.

I peeled off my right glove and reached out, and I touched the tears on his cheek, and I saw his eyes go wide and I saw him see me.

"I'm here," I said.

"Yes," he sighed.

We were in sync again.

I held out my hand, pulled him to his feet.

There was no time to try to understand what had just happened.

"Listen," said Lars.

I listened.

"You hear that?" said Lars.

"Yes," I said.

It was a dog barking somewhere, far away.

"That's not good, is it?" said Lars.

"No," I said.

I listened again. The dog was coming closer.

There was not much we could do if someone was hunting us. If we were still in Rebecca's world and the people who were out there, hunting us, had set their dogs loose in the woods. There was nowhere to hide and no way to outrun the dogs in the snow.

But there was a tree right in front of us. We could climb it.

"We have to go up," I said.

"All right," said Lars. He knew enough now about the strange new world he was in not to waste any time asking questions.

We went to the wet and wretched tree in front of us, and found slippery footholds and damp handholds and scrambled up until we were sitting in the branches, swaying slightly, ten feet above the path.

I could hear the dog, clearer now, coming closer through the trees.

Then there was a pattering sound and we looked down. The sleek black shape of a Dobermann came upon our footprints in the snow. It wasn't barking anymore. It had caught a scent. It sniffed at the ground, rooting around where we had walked, and then it looked up and sniffed the air and cocked its head to look right at us.

I could hardly breathe.

It didn't bark. It didn't growl or bare its teeth.

What it did was—it wagged its tail.

A man was coming toward us through the snow. We could hear him calling his dog.

"Oskar! . . . Oskar! . . . Oskar!"

The man appeared in the clearing below us.

"There you are."

Oskar barked.

The man looked up at us.

"Hello," I said. "We're afraid of your dog."

"Oh," said the man. "You don't have to be scared of silly old Oskar. He's a sweetheart."

But he put Oskar on the leash anyway, and we climbed down from the tree.

A jogger came running past us and we all had to get out of his way because he wasn't going to deviate from his course one inch. Then we asked the man with the dog if there was a bus stop anywhere near here and he said yes, just up there at the top of the hill.

"Follow the path and you can't go wrong," he said.

Forty-six

There were streetlights and skyglow and a bus waiting at the stop, and we ran for it with cold, tired legs.

"See," I said to Lars as we stepped on to the bus. "I told you we weren't lost."

The bus pulled away and we went for seats at the back, swaying, and just as we sat down my cell phone vibrated in my pocket.

I took it out and looked at the screen.

Mom calling.

I had to answer it.

"Hello?" I said.

"Kara. Where are you?"

"On the bus on the way home," I said. "I'll be home in ten minutes."

"Are you alone?" Mom asked.

"Yes," I said. Then I thought it might be better if I was with someone if I was out so late, so I said, "No. I'm with someone."

Lars looked at me and grinned.

"Who are you with?" said Mom.

"Um . . . A friend," I said.

Lars and I looked at each other awkwardly.

"Have you been fighting?" said Mom.

"Fighting? No," I said. "No, really everything's OK."

That was the truth. For the first time in a long time, it felt like everything was going to be OK.

I walked Lars home. He was silent, shaken up. His world had changed.

We said good-bye, and then I walked back up the Viking Steps to my apartment building.

It started to snow right then. Great big flakes drifted down through the dark to the earth.

I let myself into the lobby. I thought about Rebecca who had died, and I thought about Samuel who had lived.

Something woke me in the night and when I opened my eyes there was a sliver of blue light blinking at my bedroom window.

I got out of bed and went to the window and looked out.

There was an ambulance parked in the courtyard of one of the buildings below, its blue light blinking furiously. Two paramedics were stretchering an old man into the open doors at the back. The old man had an oxygen mask over his nose and his eyes were closed. He looked pale, too pale, I thought, and I wondered if he was going to die.

One of the paramedics climbed into the back with the old man. The other one closed the doors and got in the front. The ambulance turned quickly in the courtyard and snaked its way between the apartment buildings back to the main road, and then I heard the siren coming on.

They were in a hurry. Which meant the old man was in trouble. I wondered whether he would make it. I wondered if he had people who cared about him. People who were worried about him.

If anybody would miss him if he died in the night.

Forty-seven

The next day I was hurrying past the garages at the bottom of the Viking Steps when something weird happened.

I heard a noise, a creaking noise, and something emerged from the mouth of the garages ahead of me and rolled across the ice and grit, until it came to a stop right in front of me.

For a moment I couldn't make out what I was looking at.

It was an old wheelchair with a black seat and a dull metal frame. Someone had parked it—or abandoned it—in one of the garages, and the brake must have slipped off just as I was walking by.

I wondered whose it was and who had left it here.

I put my hands on the handles and turned it and trundled it back into the garages, crossing the line from the street into the gloom. I found the brake pedal at the back of the wheelchair and locked it, and went back out into the daylight.

Then I realized where I was. Right in front of me was the apartment building where I'd seen footprints in the snow on the roof.

This was where the ambulance had been last night.

I went up to the entrance, right up to the glass in the lobby door, and cupped my hands around my eyes and peered into the gloom. I could see a long row of metal mailboxes on the wall, but it was impossible to read any of the names from where I stood. I wondered about the old man I'd seen last night. I wondered who he was.

I wondered who the wheelchair belonged to.

I went to the public library. I had a hunch about Samuel Liederman.

I asked a librarian how I could find out if he'd survived and where he lived.

She helped me. We couldn't find his name on any lists of refugees arriving in Great Britain toward the end of the war. But to my amazement we did find a Mr. Samuel Liederman living in Sweden.

He lived in Stockholm. I gasped when I saw the address.

It was the apartment building just down the hill.

Lars came with me. We waited outside the address I'd been given by the librarian. It was the apartment building closest to the lake, with the best views year round.

This was one building Lars didn't know the door code for, so we lingered outside.

It was cold, and we waited.

The door opened and a middle-aged woman came out and glanced at us, and went on her way. But as soon as her back was turned Lars wheeled away from me and caught the door just as it was swinging shut.

He caught it silently and held it.

I went through the open door.

I looked at the names on the mailboxes in the lobby.

One name jumped out at me: LIEDERMAN, S.

LIEDERMAN, S. lived on the seventh floor.

We took the elevator up. There were only two apartments up there. The door to one of the apartments was open. I could see into the hallway inside. There were boxes—packing boxes—on the floor.

I looked at the name on the mailbox.

Liederman, S.

This was it.

Behind us somebody called the elevator and it began to descend.

I knocked on the door.

"Hello?" I said.

We went into the apartment.

"Is there anybody home?" I said.

"Hello!" said Lars.

Some of the boxes were sealed, and others were only half-full and open.

Somebody was moving out, I thought.

Lars went on ahead of me and I stopped. There was a door ajar to my left, and when I peered in through the crack I saw a small, tidy bedroom with a large closet in the far corner. I was about to look away when something odd happened.

There was a creaking noise and, slowly, the closet door swung open.

I recognized something in the closet.

Something blue.

Something old.

I pushed the bedroom door open and went in. I stepped carefully over the open boxes on the floor and went to the closet.

It was what I thought it was.

It was the old blue coat.

Samuel, I thought.

I reached out and touched it. It felt rough and worn but still somehow strong and warm. It was a hundred years old now if it was a day. Samuel had been wearing it when he'd been rescued. He'd kept it all these years.

My hands brushed over something in one of the pockets. A little bump.

I slipped my hand into the pocket and felt the object inside.

The old tin whistle.

I held it in my hand for a moment.

Then I blew on it, once, and put it back where it belonged.

"It's him," I said when I went into the main room.

"I know," said Lars.

There was a wheelchair parked in a corner.

There were large picture windows facing north and west, wrapped around the corner of the building. They afforded panoramic views of Lake Mälaren and the woods beyond, and of the island a little farther away.

The lake was still frozen.

"Here," said Lars. He'd spied an old black-and-white photograph in a plain wooden frame on the windowsill.

I went over to him and looked at it.

It was Samuel in the photograph. As I knew him, as a child. He was seated, of course, to hide his disability. But he was not alone. Beside him, sitting with him, was Rebecca. And beside her was another child, an older sister. And behind them were their parents, smiling, proud, and alongside them and around them were their grandparents, and two aunts, and a single uncle, and two dogs and a black-and-white cat.

The photograph had been taken in happier days, before the soldiers came.

Of them all, only Samuel had survived.

These were the disappeared. These were the people the soldiers had rounded up, that day when Rebecca and Samuel were playing in the cellar. These people who numbered among the six million dead.

There were footsteps behind us and we turned, and heard a man's voice saying, "Who's there? Is there somebody there?"

"In here," I said quickly. "Sorry. We were looking for Samuel Liederman."

A man entered. A young man in a dark suit, about thirty years old, tall, with dark hair.

It was not Samuel Liederman.

"Who are you?" he said.

"Sorry," I said. "I—I'm Kara Lukas. I was looking for Mr. Liederman. The door was open, so I . . ."

I trailed off. "Sorry," I said, "I realize that we shouldn't have come in."

"Are you a friend of Mr. Liederman's?" the man asked.

I was silent for a moment, and then I said, "Yes."

It was true.

"Yes," I said. "I am a friend of his."

The young man nodded.

"In that case I have some rather sad news," he said. "I'm afraid Mr. Liederman died two days ago. The funeral has already taken place. My name is Mr. Sanderson. I'm the family lawyer and the executor of the will."

Two days.

My mind was racing.

We'd missed him by two days.

I remembered the ambulance parked outside this very building. The flashing blue light. The sound of a siren blipping up through the air.

Two paramedics stretchering an old man into the back of the ambulance and spiriting him away . . .

An old man called Samuel Liederman.

Another ghost.

Tears were shining in my eyes.

The lawyer looked at me with concern.

"Are you going to be all right?"

"Yes," I said.

"I'm sorry you missed the funeral," he said. "Mr. Liederman is buried in the Jewish cemetery at Aronsberg . . . if you'd like to pay your respects."

"Yes," I said, "I'd like that."

Lars and I went to Aronsberg. The gates of the old cemetery were locked, but Mr. Liederman's lawyer had given us the cell-phone number of the caretaker who looked after the place. We called him now, and a few minutes later he came out of an apartment building nearby.

He was a young Black man named Joseph and he unlocked the gates ("Too many bad people around for us to leave the place unlocked," he said, "even here in Stockholm.") and took us inside, placing a yarmulke on his head as he did so. Then he took another one out of his pocket and offered it to Lars, explaining that this small circular cap is meant to be worn by all men in places that are sacred to Judaism.

"I think you should wear it," said Joseph.

Lars nodded and took it from him and covered his head.

I took out the small map the lawyer had drawn for us but when I said the name Samuel Liederman, Joseph smiled and said, "I know where it is," and we followed him along the path between the snow-covered stones.

The memorial stone was new and lay flat on the ground. Once we'd wiped the snow off, we saw that it said simply, LIEDERMAN, followed by words in Hebrew.

Small stones had been placed on the grave.

I'd brought stones for us to leave here too.

Lars took something out of his pocket. It was an obituary he'd found in a Stockholm daily newspaper.

It told us everything we needed to know.

Samuel's plane never made it back to England. They were attacked over Denmark. They went down in flames in the sea between Sweden and Germany. But they all had life jackets, even Samuel, and they bobbed up and down in the water. They drifted north to a Swedish beach: the current had carried them to safety.

The British pilot and crew were sent to a prisoner-of-war camp; that was the end of the war for them.

Samuel was sent by night train, alone, to Stockholm, where his aunt, Emma Liederman, was waiting for him. She was twenty years old and living in a small apartment in one of the poorer parts of town. But they knew, even before it was confirmed by the refugee agencies at the end of the war, that they were the only ones in their family who had survived. They were all that remained of the Liedermans.

They were all they had in the world.

Samuel stayed with Emma in Stockholm. He was married here. He had children here. One of his children—a girl—was named Rebecca.

She has children of her own now.

It's survival, I thought. *It's enough. It's everything.*

Lars folded the obituary and put it away.

I reached into my pocket and took out two small round smooth stones. They were from the sea. I'd collected them on a beach in southern Sweden, years ago. It seemed appropriate to leave them here now. They'd been worn down by the waves and dashed against other stones, but they'd survived.

I gave Lars his stone and he placed it on the grave.

I looked at the stone in my hand.

I placed it soundlessly on Samuel Liederman's grave.

It would remain there for as long as there was a Joseph, or someone like him, to keep watch over the graves.

Forty-eight

The next morning there was a message from Rebecca in the snow.

I opened the blinds and looked out on the sunlit snowed-in city.

Somebody had been on the rooftops again.

Somebody had made a smiley face in the snow on the roof of one of the apartment buildings below.

Two big eyes and an even bigger smile.

Forty-nine

Somewhere out there in the woods there was a coin under the snow, waiting to be found. A coin with an eagle and a swastika on it.

But I didn't want to find it.

I knew enough.

Lars thinks I'm a hero but I know I'm not. I did the one small thing I'd promised a friend I'd do, that's all. I was brave at the right moment, and I had my wits about me, but I'm not a hero.

I'm no more extraordinary than you would be if you'd discovered an island in time. If you met a child who needed your help. If you met Rebecca.

If there's a hero here it's Rebecca. She saved us all. She saved Samuel by hiding him, feeding him, keeping him warm, collecting wood, picking berries, keeping his spirits up, telling him stories. She saved him thousands of times.

And she saved me. She saved me from myself, from my loneliness. She saved me from being alone.

She was my friend.

She was my friend, and I couldn't save her.

All I could do was be there when she died. So she didn't die alone. So she died with a friend at her side.

Someone who loved her.

Fifty

There was another funeral a few days later. Mom and I, and a few distant relatives, and those friends of his who were still alive, went out to the Forest Cemetery in Stockholm to say farewell to David Lukas, my grandpa.

It was a simple, dignified service. Grandpa lay in a plain wood coffin.

Mom spoke about his kindness.

I spoke about his love of astronomy.

I said I hoped he was stardust now.

When the ushers opened the doors at the end of the service, we saw snow falling thickly and silently.

Snow was falling over all of Sweden they said on the weather forecast.

I looked at the chimney above the crematorium.

A thin strand of smoke rose, and the snow fell.

We hadn't decided yet what to do with his ashes.

Fifty-one

Mom and I were decluttering. We were at Grandpa's house going through the last of his things, deciding what to keep and what, finally, to give away.

Grandpa had made many of the decisions for us. He had embarked on the big project of decluttering his entire life; he just hadn't quite finished it when he died.

We were in the attic. We'd created piles below, on the landing: one for keeps, one for recycling, one for the thrift shops. Some of the decisions were easy. Others were impossible.

We got stuck on the same things Grandpa got stuck on.

My grandma's things.

Her clothes. Her pretty dresses. Her notebooks, which were filled with stories she'd invented for my mother when she was a little girl and had written down, by hand. Her maps, which she collected, of faraway places, some of which she visited, some of which remained, to her at least, imaginary. Her ice skates.

Her name was Kara. She died before I was born, although Mom says she lived long enough to be told I was on the way, to put her hand on Mom's belly, and to learn that I would share her name if I was a girl.

I was a girl. So Kara it is.

"Let's keep all these things for now," said Mom.

"Yes," I said.

I put the other Kara's dresses back in their paper covers and stowed them away in the trunk at the far end of the crawl space.

Mom was rummaging around behind me.

"There was a blue coat," she said, "a big old blue coat I had when I was a teenager. I don't think Grandpa would have thrown it out."

Her hands moved quickly through an old trunk.

"He didn't throw it out," I said. "I took it."

She looked at me.

"Grandpa let me."

"OK," she said. "Where is it?"

"I don't have it."

"Kara, where is it?"

"My friend has it," I said. "The one I told you about. I gave it to her. She was cold and she needed a big winter coat, and it was just right."

Mom nodded. "Is she doing all right, now? Your friend. Is she OK?"

I didn't really know what to say, so I lied. "She's fine," I said. "She, um, she moved away, so I don't know if I'll see her again."

"So we're never going to get that coat back," said Mom.

I groaned. I was at a loss.

"Don't worry about it," said Mom. "It doesn't matter. I was going to give you that coat anyway. If it helped someone out one winter, so much the better."

She looked at her watch. "Let's go down and get some lunch," she said. As she was climbing down through the hatch I said, "Everything's going to be all right, you know," and she stopped and looked at me.

"I know," she said. "There's just the two of us now, but . . ."

"We're going to be all right," I said, finishing her sentence for her.

"That's because you're you," she said, "and you're a star. But things might have been very different. You might not have been you, and things might have been difficult for the 'you' you turned out to be. It might have been a problem for you, not having a dad, or not having a little brother or sister, or . . ."

It's not a problem. I have friends. I'm OK.

"But you seem to have thrived," she said. "You seem—I don't know—somehow even braver than you were before. I can see my mother in you—your grandma. I can see her fearlessness in you. And that's why I know we're going to be all right."

Even braver than I was before. Fearless. That's me.

Mom smiled and said, "I'm going to go and make some lunch now before I cry."

I nodded. "I'll finish up here," I said.

She went down.

I put Grandma's ice skates away in the trunk alongside her notebooks, the ones she'd filled with her stories. My hands lingered on the edge of the lid of the trunk. I could feel the notebooks watching me, daring me to take the first one off the top of the pile and open it and start reading what was written there.

"Another time, Kara," I said.

I closed the lid.

Fifty-two

Someone had made a snow angel in a great bank of snow down by the lake. There was something wrong with it and I knew what it was.

There were no footprints. No footprints leading to it and no footprints leading away from it.

This time though, I knew how it was done. I knew because I did it. I made it.

I made the snow angel.

With Lars, who has become my accomplice.

This is how we did it. We got hold of a long piece of rope. We threw it up over a branch. We tied one end to another branch, and tied a knot in it for a foothold. Then because I was the lightest, I swung on the rope, to and fro, back and forth over a big snowdrift we'd found, with Lars pushing me farther and farther.

I let go.

I landed in the middle of the drift, and Lars caught the rope as it swung back toward him. I lay down and made a snow angel. When I was done, Lars swung the rope back to me and I caught it and hitched myself up on it and let the rope carry me back to Lars, who caught me.

Mystery solved.

From the woods that day we went down to the lake.

It was the last day before school. The holidays were over. I wanted one last look at the island.

We skated out on the lake. Crows watched us from the trees.

We came to the island. I breathed in the cold air. There was no scent in the air of bonfire smoke.

They're gone, I thought. *Good.*

I heard a voice. "Kara?"

It was Rebecca's voice, and I didn't believe what I'd heard, but I turned, and there she was. She looked exactly as she did the first time I saw her.

She had a bundle of twigs and branches under her arm, wood for a fire.

I was lost for words.

"Are you cold?" she asked. "It's a cold day. I'm going to make a fire. Come and get warm."

Still I couldn't say anything. I stared at her.

"Your friend is welcome, too," she said with a nod of her head toward Lars.

Lars looked at me and nodded. He saw her, too.

Rebecca had seen the look between us. She frowned. She began to wonder about my silence. My surprise. She wondered why I was looking at her like I'd seen a ghost.

"Oh!" Her hands flew to her mouth and she dropped the wood she was carrying. It clattered on to the ice.

"It's happened, hasn't it?" she said.

I nodded.

I had tears in my eyes.

Rebecca nodded. Then she said, "Is he safe? Is Samuel safe?"

I nodded again and Rebecca smiled.

"Then I can go on my way through the universe."

That broke me.

That cut right through me. I cried.

"That's right," I said to her through tears, "you can go on your way."

This had been her burden. Her choice, her task. To keep Samuel alive, even if it meant becoming a ghost herself. To save a life, even if it meant lingering in the living world, like light from a distant star that had already been extinguished.

Rebecca smiled again, or tried to smile, but the tears came anyway, running silently down her cheeks, and I understood how lonely she was, how lonely she'd been, how she'd needed my friendship even more than I'd needed hers.

"Will you think of me?" she said.

"I'll think of you," I said.

"Will you remember me?"

"I'll remember you," I said. "I promise I'll remember you. When I look up at the stars that are older than us all. The stars that shone on you and still shine down on me. I'll remember you when I look up at the sky, the sky we shared, the sky over Rebecca . . . My sky. Our sky."

She came to me and kissed me on the cheek, and we hugged and held our embrace for a long time.

"Good-bye, Kara," she whispered in my ear.

"Good-bye, Rebecca," I whispered back.

She drew back.

Lars had picked up the wood she'd dropped on the ice and bundled it up for her. Now she took it from him and walked away from us, toward the island.

Lars said, "That's her, isn't it? That's Rebecca."

"That's her," I said.

She disappeared into the trees.

That was the last time I ever saw her.

"How can we help her?" said Lars.

I thought about his question for a long time. I wanted to say, *We can't help her, no one can, because it's already happened.* I wanted to say, *We can stop this ever happening again, we can refuse to forget.* But as my thoughts went on twisting and churning, I realized there was one more thing we could do for Rebecca.

One more thing we had to do.

Fifty-three

Nautical twilight.

All the windows of the old house were dark.

Lars and I came crunching through the snow. I used my key in the door and we went in. I went to the storeroom in the kitchen and took out a candle and a box of matches.

"There's a letter for you," said Lars.

I came back. There was a white envelope on the kitchen table with my name on it.

It was my grandpa's handwriting, and underneath my name he'd added, "Not to be opened until your next birthday."

Mom must have found it, among Grandpa's papers, and left it here for me.

"When's your birthday?" Lars said.

"December," I said.

"That's almost a year away," said Lars.

"Yes," I said. But I wasn't going to open it before then. I picked up the envelope and felt it. It was heavier than just a card. There was a letter inside, probably.

He knew he didn't have long to live. He wanted to get his thoughts down on paper for me. I was happy to wait almost a year to read them.

I put the kettle on and made two hot chocolates from packages I'd found in the cupboard. We sat at the kitchen table and drank them while we waited for it to get fully dark.

I remembered what had happened in this room the last time I was here, when I'd had a conversation about ghosts with a ghost.

I didn't tell Lars about that.

Some experiences are best kept to yourself.

We went out into the garden.

It was darker than before, the sky another shade of blue-black above us with a faint orange hue over the city in the east.

Astronomical twilight.

The stars were out.

We went down through the snow to the old jetty jutting out on the frozen lake.

We stepped on to the wood, which creaked underneath us. We went to the end of the jetty and sat down. The ice was solid and weirdly flat. Like it was all a single piece of white stone that had been polished by time and tides.

Lars held the candle.

I struck a match, and it flared briefly and went out. I struck another and it flared, stronger, and stayed alight long enough for me to get the candle lit.

Lars cupped his hands around the flame, sheltering it.

We looked out across the lake.

There was no one out there we could see.

A breath of wind swept across the lake toward us. The trees on the far shore swayed. Snow scurried in little squalls across the perfectly flat ice.

The candle flame shivered for a moment and guttered, and we thought we'd lost it, but it held.

It stayed alight, sheltered by our hands.

The wind dropped away to nothing. We looked out into the white gloom of the lake.

"Is she out there, do you think?" said Lars.

"She's out there," I said.

"I hope she sees us," he said.

"She sees us," I said.

We held the candle for her.

Acknowledgments

A book needs help to find its way into the real world—and I have a lot of people to thank.

To my agent Lauren Gardner at Bell Lomax Moreton, thank you for your support, your suggestions, and your tireless efforts on behalf of this book. I know very well I would not be writing these words without your hard work, and I am in your debt.

To my editors, Anne McNeil and Jenna Mackintosh, and to the entire team at Hodder, thank you for your willingness to take a chance on a first-time author. Your patience, your care, and your wise edits have made this a much better book than it would otherwise have been.

To Caroline Ambrose, thank you for creating the Bath Children's Novel Award, which has helped so many new writers find agents and publishers. We would be lost without you. And a special thank you to the Junior Judges, who chose to put this book on the shortlist. Keep reading, and keep writing. I hope to read the books you write some day.

To my friends in Liverpool, Stockholm, and Cape Town, thank you for so many long conversations over the years about screenwriting and storytelling. I'm a better writer because of your insights. I'm a better person because of your friendship.

To Julieann and Dom, thank you for being there at the (new) beginning.

To my father, thank you for the gift of reading and writing. You did not live to see this book in print, but I think somehow you always knew it would happen.

To Aaron Hicklin, thank you for showing the way. Your energy is a liberation.

And finally, to Ulrica and Kay, thank you for making my world anew.

Photograph © Julieann O'Malley

Matthew Fox grew up in Wiltshire, England, and now lives in Stockholm, Sweden with his partner and child. He studied at the University of Oxford and the Northern Film School. His first novel for children, *The Sky Over Rebecca*, won the Bath Children's Novel Award 2019.

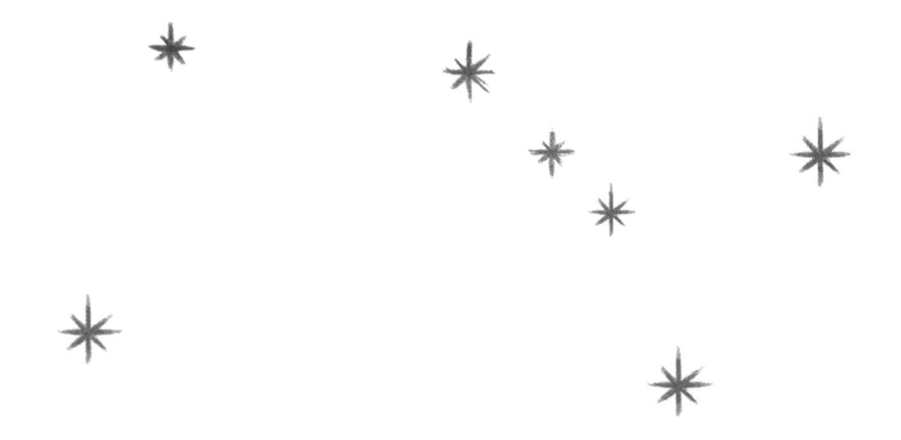

A friendship across time

A story written in the stars